Diane Williams Gordon

Return to
Ruby Hope Valley

Black Rose Writing | Texas

ISBN: 978-1-68433-516-9
PUBLISHED BY BLACK ROSE WRITING
www.blackrosewriting.com

Printed in the United States of America
Suggested Retail Price (SRP) $18.95

Return to Ruby Hope Valley is printed in Palatino Linotype

*As a planet-friendly publisher, Black Rose Writing does its best to eliminate
unnecessary waste to reduce paper usage and energy costs, while never compromising
the reading experience. As a result, the final word count vs. page count may not meet
common expectations.

Acknowledgment

I wish to acknowledge my publisher, Reagan Rothe at Black Rose Writing. I would also like to thank my children for encouraging me to write these stories of Ruby Hope Valley and for their support and inspiration. I want to thank my husband, Jerry, for his patience and understanding through all the long hours of working on this novel.

I would also like to dedicate this novel to my Mother, Ruby Williams, from whom the title of the books were named after. Her love has been my inspiration through this whole process.

I have always been intrigued by the everyday culture of the Amish people. Their plain and simple ways of life. The strong bonds they have with their community and commitment to family has fascinated me for years.

Diane Williams Gordon's first novel, *Ruby Hope Valley* has received some wonderful praise, like the two reviews featured below, on many different reading platforms.

"A Sweet story filled with hope, love and possibilities. Where a lonely woman join's an Amish quilting group, she finds so much more than friendship. She finds joy in living a simpler life, purpose and acceptance into an Amish family. So tender and touching."

"A Wonderful Read. I just finished reading *Ruby Hope Valley*. I enjoyed the book from start to finish. A beautiful story."

Ruby Hope Valley was selected by BookBub for an International Featured Deal, where it reached number one for the day on August 11, 2019. The novel was an international hit in Australia, Canada and the United Kingdom.

Return to
Ruby Hope Valley

Prologue

Return to Ruby Hope Valley is a continuation of Betty Anne and Sara Jane's children and grandchildren. Their hopes and dreams for the future.

Joseph Levi and Samuel John face difficulties as they become adults and the Orphan children learn to love the Amish way of life. Joseph Levi longs to become a Veterinarian as Samuel John has a tragic accident that changes his life.

The children strive to overcome their difficulties and continue their lives with the love, support, and strength of family. The support of the Amish community; and the caring people of Ruby Hope Valley.

A story of faith, hope, and love; a story of true friendship

Chapter One

It was 6 am on a cool fall morning when Levi entered the barn. As he bailed hay for the cows his mind rambled on about his sons. He knew they had different ambitions they wanted to pursue, but he was just a typical Amish man. He spoke out loud in the silence of the morning. "I just want my sons to follow in my footsteps; and become a blacksmith like me and my father before me. Joseph Levi's heart desire is to become a veterinarian one day: and that's all he's ever wanted to do. I'm worried about him because of his eighth-grade education. The boys desire to become a veterinarian may never become a reality."

As Levi walked back to the house in the cool mist morning for breakfast, he thought about Samuel John and how he loved to ride horses. So, he decided to give him a horse of his own. As they sat down for breakfast, Levi looked over at Samuel John and said. "Son, you are twelve years old now and old enough to take good care of a horse. So, I have decided to give you Abby." Samuel John's eyes lit up like a firecracker. "Oh father, do you mean it; I can have Abby for my very own?"

"Yes son, but you better take good care of her or I will take her away from thee."

"I will obey thee, father because I love Abby. I will take very good care of her. You will see father."

Samuel John brushed her down every day when he wasn't riding her. The farmers along the main road that leads into the next little town of Morganville saw him riding the horse often.

The horse could run very fast and Samuel John would push her to the limit. He would sneak out of the house while the family was asleep and ride the horse late at night. He rode the horse as fast as she could take him. He loved the wind in his face and the thrill of the speed the horse could go. Joseph Levi and Jacob knew that Samuel John was going out at night to ride the horse. He knew they wouldn't tell on him.

Late one night, Abby came too close to the edge of the road and slipped down a ravine.

He was thrown off his horse and landed in the dirt. He was face down in the mud as blood ran out of his nose. The poor horse lay in the ravine with a torn ankle, bleeding profusely. Samuel John wasn't discovered until the next morning. A neighbor, Mr. Seth whose farm was just down the road from the Click family, was out walking that morning when he discovered Samuel John lying in the road.

"Help, help, someone please help us?" As he called for help, he began to shake and tremble as Samuel John looked as though he wasn't breathing. Some of the other neighbors came running down the road to see what happened to the boy. Martha Fisher ran down to the field where the public phone booth was located and phoned for an ambulance.

Jonathan Fisher got in his horse-drawn buggy and rode to the Click farm to tell Levi and Sara Jane about their son.

When Sara Jane and Levi arrived at the spot where their son was lying in the road, they jumped down from the buggy and ran over to him. His mama began to scream and cry out.

"Samuel John, Samuel John, please wake up." Levi laid his son's head on his lap. Samuel John was still breathing, but it was very shallow; they could see blood coming from his mouth and nose. The ambulance arrived and lifted him onto a stretcher as his mama and dad climbed into the back of the ambulance with him.

"Martha, would you please call Betty Anne for me and let her know what happened.

Her phone number is sitting on the kitchen table. What am I going to do about Cindy and Daisy?"

"Don't you worry now Sara Jane I will take care of the girls for you."

Sara Jane was grateful to Martha and thanked her for being there for her.

Betty Anne answered the phone and realized it was Martha Fisher. Martha explained to her about Samuel John. "Thank you for calling Martha and letting me know about Samuel John." As she hung up the phone, she began to pray, *"Please God help Samuel John be ok and bless the family."* After arriving at the hospital, Betty Anne heard someone say Samuel John was in critical condition. The tears started rolling down her cheeks as she tried to control herself for Sara Jane and Levi's sake. She had known this boy since he was born and couldn't imagine being without him. After all, he was like a grandson.

Martha Fisher climbed in her buggy and drove to the Click farm. She told the children what happened to Samuel John. "What is going to happen to him, Martha?"

"Cindy, it's in God's hands now, and only he knows." She helped the girls get ready for school and made them breakfast. Joseph Levi and Jacob were out of school now and knew Levi would want them to continue their work on the farm. When Samuel came into work that day, the boys told him what happened to their brother. Joseph Levi said. "Samuel, will you go with us to see about the horse? As far as we know, Abby is still lying in the ravine."

Samuel was worried about Samuel John, but he knew Levi would want him to stay on the farm with the boys. There was always so much work to do in the barn, and he didn't want to leave them alone around the blacksmith forge. Samuel said. "Hitch up the horse and buggy, and we will go see about Abby." In the back of Samuel's mind, he was afraid he was going to find the horse dead or with a broken leg. He knew he might have to put the horse down.

By now everyone in the community had heard the news about the child's accident. Several of the Amish families drove to the hospital to give prayer and support to Sara Jane and Levi. There was so many horse and buggies coming down the road; it looked like a convoy approaching the town. The folks of Ruby Hope had heard about the little Amish boy and began organizing a collection to pay his hospital bills. This town had the most caring people; they were always there for one another.

Chapter Two

Levi and Sara Jane were devastated as they sat waiting for the Doctor. They held hands while they prayed for Samuel John. *"Dear Lord, please help our son be alright and give us the strength we need to go on."* It wasn't long before Betty Anne arrived at the hospital. "I've been praying for Samuel John. I want you'll to know I love you; and will always be here for you."

"Betty Anne, Samuel John was thrown off his horse and is in critical condition." The two women sat down together and put their arms around one another.

It wasn't long before several Amish families from the community came to the hospital.

They were there to give support and prayer to the couple. Levi said. "I am so grateful for all our friends." After several hours of waiting, the doctor arrived to give an update on Samuel John.

Samuel, Joseph Levi, and Jacob went down the road in the buggy to see where the accident took place. They found Abby still lying in a ravine off the road. The horse had been lying there all night and half the next day.

Abby couldn't get up, so Samuel went down the hill and coaxed her to her feet. "Come on girl, get up, get up Abby, you can do it." Suddenly, Abby rose to her feet, holding one of her legs up. He thought for sure her leg was broken, especially the way she was holding it up.

"Jacob, Joseph Levi go hitch Abby up to the back of the buggy, I want to get a better look at that leg she keeps holding up."

Abby followed behind the buggy limping, holding her leg up as much as she could until they reached the barn. Samuel guided the horse inside the barn and brushed her down; and gave her some water. He knelt and examined her leg. He couldn't feel any broken bones in the leg but it seemed very sensitive to the touch. Samuel decided rather than to put the horse down, he would wrap the leg up tight and hope it was merely a sprain. Samuel desperately wanted to save the horse for Samuel John.

Joseph Levi and Jacob knew Samuel might have to shoot the horse. Both boys had a delayed response to Samuel. Stalling for time, they decided to help Samuel with Abby.

Joseph Levi started stuttering and growing flustered as he said to Jacob. Looking down and pushing his hair away from his face. "I feel guilty not telling dad about Samuel John going out at night. We should confess to dad that we knew." Looking pale, Jacob agreed with him and said. "You're right; we should tell dad what we knew." Taking a pained deep breath, Jacob said. "No matter what the consequences are."

Doctor Huddleston asked Sara Jane and Levi to step into his office so that they could talk. He took a deep breath and said. "It's feared that Samuel John may have fallen on his head, and some spinal cord injuries have occurred. Now some of these injuries are permanent, and some are temporary. He may have just bruised his spine. We won't know until further examination has been done on the boy. He may lose muscle function, and function in other parts of his body, as well. I don't know the extent of the injuries just yet, but I am hoping it's only temporary until he regains the function of his body. It's going to take time."

Sara Jane turned away and covered her mouth. She felt like she was going to start screaming at any moment. "No, it's not true, this can't be happening to our son. Are you sure Doctor?" Levi and Sara Jane's thoughts were scrambling to understand the situation. "I just can't believe this." She repeated herself over and over. "I can't understand this with tears streaming down her face." Levi was beside himself and tried to console Sara Jane."

"We have to be brave and pray for our son to get better." She tried to be brave, but the tears would not stop.

After several weeks in the hospital, Samuel John began to regain some of his body functions. The doctor was confident that he would be able to walk again. Doctor Huddleston said. "Don't give up hope on the boy; he seems to be getting a little feeling back in some parts of his body. The paralyzes may only be temporary, and it's going to take time." Betty

Anne hugged Sarah Jane and said. "Don't you worry; God has this in his hands."

The nurses would get Samuel John up every morning and take him to therapy in a wheelchair. A nurse would work with him until his strength was gone. Sara Jane and Levi would visit him every day. They knew he was scared, and this was the first time he had ever been away from home. Doctor Huddleston and the nurses tried to explain to Samuel John what had happened to him. Nurse Gray spoke up and said to Samuel John, "You were thrown off your horse and landed on your head and neck. You see that is the reason you are having trouble moving your arms and legs." He still didn't understand and kept saying he just wanted to go home.

A young girl named Betsy came by every day to see him and read him a Bible story. She was a candy stripe girl whose duties were to make sure all the children patients were happy and comfortable being away from home. She would entertain them by reading stories or playing games with them. Samuel John really liked her and looked forward to her visits. When Betsy got off work, she would go by the library to pick up some Amish Christian books to read to Samuel John. Betsy said. "I have a little brother at home, and I know how scary it must be for children to be away from their families." He would smile at her and say, "I want to go home and see my horse."

He looked forward to seeing his mama and dad every day. He told them about Betsy and how she came every morning to read him an Amish story. Sara Jane was so grateful and wanted to thank her for reading to Samuel John. It wasn't long before she came into his room. Betsy was very young and had a pleasant smile. She looked to be sixteen at the most. "Thank you for being so nice to our son; he enjoys your visits."

The days, weeks and months that followed were critical for Samuel John. He had signs of improvement, but it would still be a long time before he would walk again. Doctor Huddleston said frowning. "Levi, Sara Jane, I won't lie to you. The paralyzes Samuel John has could only be temporary, but we don't know yet. He's moving his arms and legs, and it looks as if he is better." The doctor was searching for the right words to say to these people. He needed reassurance himself. "He still needs a lot of therapy, and that's what we're trying to do for him."

He had been in the hospital for almost four months, and his mama and dad couldn't understand why he wasn't walking yet. They prayed each day with Samuel John. "We want you to come home, but you must be patient, and let the doctors and nurses help you get well." His little face would wrinkle up, and tears would start rolling down his cheeks; he just wanted to go home.

Chapter Three

The months and weeks that followed were long and frustrating for the boy. The weather outside had begun to get cold, and soon the snow would once again come to Ruby Hope Valley.

No one could remember a winter in the past ten years when it didn't snow. Samuel John looked out the window of his hospital room and watched the white snowflakes come down. He reminisced about the farm and how he and his brothers would throw snowballs at each other and chase each other across the snowy fields. He longed to be home on the farm with his family and cried until he fell asleep.

Snow continued to come down as October sneaked into November. It was almost Thanksgiving and Samuel John was still in the hospital. Betty Anne was asked to come out to the farm and join them for Thanksgiving. She decided she would get a big turkey and take it to her friend to cook. Sara Jane's heart just wasn't in the cooking mood this year. "I know I need to be strong for the family, but I'm having a hard time getting started. My heart isn't into cooking right now. I am grateful Betty Anne, for the nice turkey. I'll get it in the wood stove right away."

She asked Cindy to get more firewood off the back porch for her. After the stove was heated, she put the turkey in a big pot and rubbed it all over with melted butter. She then put together a homemade dressing of dried breadcrumbs Sautéed onion, celery, dried thyme, dried parsley, ground rosemary, dried marjoram, and salt and pepper. She mixed this all together and placed it inside the turkey. Sara Jane began to put together a delicious Thanksgiving dinner. As she cooked for the family; her spirits began to rise. As she was preparing the food, she thought of Samuel John and was hopeful he would be home next Thanksgiving.

A Poem by Orva Hochstetler, written May 1, 2017

"The Love of God"
We can feel it in a soft breeze
We can see it in colored leaves
We can receive it through a friend
It will be with us in the end; it's the Love of God

Samuel John was getting better and wanted to get out of the hospital bed. One morning he attempted to get up and fail on the floor. He was able to move his upper body, but his legs were still weak, and he couldn't stand on them. He made such a clatter nurse Gray came running into the room and helped him get up off the floor. She called another nurse to bring a wheelchair for him. "You should never try to get out of bed by yourself again. You could have hurt yourself, Samuel John."

Betsy came by that morning. "How would you like for me to roll you down the hall to the waiting rooms. I will read you a new story." She could tell that he had been crying and put her arms around him. "I can't understand why I can't walk yet, Betsy." She said. "With God all things are possible, and you shouldn't worry; it's just a matter of time." He always looked forward to her stopping by and especially the stories she read to him. She made him feel at ease and comfortable. After that incident, he was afraid to try and get out of bed again.

His body was getting stronger as the days passed. The more he had the therapy, the better he felt. One afternoon the doctor stopped by to see him. "How would you like to try and walk today?" Samuel John was excited that he was going to get the chance to walk. "Are you sure doctor, I can try to walk today?" The nurse brought him two crutches to hold on too. They got him up, and he immediately started to fall. "Your legs are still weak, Samuel John, that is why you fail at first try." After a few minutes, he began moving his legs and walking very slowly across the room.

"I am amazed at how well you are doing, replied Doctor Huddleston." He turned to nurse Gray and said. "I want you to get him up every day and let him walk a little." He was a small boy for his age of twelve but very smart and determined that he was going to walk. He was anxious to get out of the bed every morning when the nurse came by to get him up. His arms and legs were getting stronger, and even though he had to use the crutches, he just knew he was going to walk one day.

He longed to go home and ride his horse. Joseph Levi and Jacob wanted to tell Levi about keeping the secret about Samuel John going out at night to ride the horse. But they knew Levi was worried about Samuel John and thought they should wait until a better time. Levi was trying to work in the shop to help keep his mind off his young son. Only Samuel knew, and he wasn't about to tell Levi; he felt that the boys should be the ones to tell him.

Samuel John had been in the hospital for six months when the doctor decided he could go home. He said. "You will have to continue going to therapy twice a week." Levi and Sara Jane was happy that Samuel John was coming home. She baked his favorite cake and made him a nice pot of vegetable soup. He loved his mama's vegetable soup and always ate two or three bowls.

The Best of Amish Cooking Recipe Book by Phyllis Pellman Good

Vegetable Beef Soup Recipe:
1 beef soup bone
2 cups peas
1 ½ tsp. salt
2 cups of green beans
2 quarts water
2 cups of corn
2 cups potatoes, peeled and diced
2 cups tomatoes or tomato juice
2 cups carrots, sliced
½ cup rice
1 cup celery, chopped
1 cup cabbage, shredded
Most all of their vegetables come from their gardens

They got up early the next day and got ready to go to the hospital to bring their son home. Levi said. "Samuel, would you watch the kids for us while we go pick Samuel John up today? Cindy and Daisy will be going to school, and Joseph Levi and Jacob will be in the barn taking care of the animals."

"Don't worry about a thing, Levi, I will be in the shop working and keeping a close eye on the two boys. They get a little rambunctious at times and I don't want anything else to happen to this family."

Samuel decided to build a ramp that would lead up to the front porch of the farmhouse.

Levi and Sara Jane could push the wheelchair up the ramp instead of having to lift it onto the porch. Samuel said. "Boys, I need your help building a ramp." They were eager to help and went into the barn to gather wood. Samuel gave them instructions on how they should build the ramp and showed them where to find the tools they needed. Joseph Levi said. "Jacob go and get the tools and bring them out to the porch. In the meantime, I will measure the distance we need to build it." Jacob brought the tools from the barn.

The boys worked all day building the ramp until they finished it. Samuel gave them a "thumbs up." He said to the boys, "That is the best-looking ramp in the county, and I am proud of you both. Sara Jane and Levi are going to be proud of you too." Before long Levi's horse, and carriage came down the dirt road. The boys ran to meet them and help them out of the carriage. They couldn't wait for Levi to see the ramp they built. Jacob said. "Dad, it will be easier to roll the wheelchair up the ramp instead of having to lift it." Levi was proud of the two boys and patted them on their backs. "You boys did a great job; it will be a big help to all of us."

Chapter Four

Samuel was still concerned about the horse. Her leg looked a lot better when he took the bandages off; but she continued to hold her leg up. Samuel thought to himself, "maybe it still hurts, and she's afraid to put it down." He had to get the horse to put pressure on her leg. So, he decided to walk her up the path; to see if she would put her leg down in the dirt. After a few minutes, Abby put her leg down and began to walk. She winched just a little then continued to walk normally. Samuel was relieved because he just knew he might have to put the horse down: He knew it would break Samuel John's heart.

Samuel took good care of the horse. Every day he changed her bandages and treated the womb with an ointment he got from the veterinarian clinic. He made a sling and put the horse's leg in it so she could take the weight off it. He would come into work earlier than usual each day so that he could check on Abby. Each day Samuel would take the horse on a little walk up the path behind the barn. Abby was getting stronger and stronger, and sometimes she would trot up the trail. Samuel had saved the animal's life and made a little boy happy.

Samuel John was so happy to be home. Cindy and Daisy came home from school and ran and hugged him. "I have missed you so much, replied Cindy." He was frustrated because he wanted to get out of the wheelchair and play with the girls. Cindy and Daisy decided they would go and get their dolls and play next to Samuel John. He sat in his wheelchair and watched the girls play and laugh. He began to feel better and started laughing along with the girls.

After a while, his mama said. "You need to lie down and rest a while, Samuel John."

Levi and Sara Jane had brought his bed down from upstairs and put it in the big sitting room. She decided to sleep on the sofa in case he needed her. He was glad his mama was going to be nearby at night because he was still frightened and didn't want to be alone.

Levi continued to take Samuel John to therapy two days a week. His legs were getting stronger each day. Doctor Huddleston warned, "Levi, please don't take the crutches away from him just yet; the child isn't ready to walk on his own." Samuel John decided one afternoon that he would like to go to the barn and visit Abby. "Joseph Levi would you help me go to the barn; I want to go see my horse." There stood Abby, big and strong as ever. He asked them to push him up close to the horse so he could pet her. Tears began to roll down his cheeks as he whispered to the horse, "I thought you were dead Abby, and I was never going to see you again. I love you so much, sweet horse."

Betty Anne heard the boy had gone home to the farm, so she decided to go visit him. As she drove down the dirt roads that lead to the Amish Community; she was in awe of all the snow-covered fields. It was February and still very cold and snowy. She had been down those same dirt roads for several years now, but she could never get over how serene and peaceful everything seemed to be. It warmed her heart to be able to be a part of these Amish people's lives. She wanted to give Samuel John a present she had been saving for him.

The girls saw her pull up and ran to greet her. She was delighted to see them since she had not been to the farm since Thanksgiving. "My goodness how you have grown, and so pretty too." They both had big smiles on their faces and grabbed her hands and led her to the front porch. She noticed Samuel John sitting on the porch in his wheelchair and gave him a big hug.

"Why are you sitting out here in the cold Samuel John?" He had a slack expression, wet, dull eyes and a trembling chin. He had been crying. "Here, let me roll you inside before we both freeze to death."

Daisy and Cindy ran into the house and said. "Mama, grandma is here." They were so excited to see her. Sara Jane ran to the door and put her arms around Betty Anne's neck. She said to her. "I am so happy to see you; you are just in time for supper." Betty Anne helped Sara Jane roll Samuel John into the house so that he could eat dinner with the family. He had drooping shoulders, a bowed spine and a sad look on his face all the time.

Betty Anne wanted to cheer him up in some way, so she brought out the compass and gave it to him. He looked at her with surprise and asked, "what is it?"

"It will help guide you wherever you go, she replied, and tell you if you are going north, south, west or east; it will always guide you home." It was small and came in a little leather pouch. Samuel John could keep it in his pocket all the time, so he would never get lost.

He was thrilled with the present and hugged her. "I love you grandma, thank you for the gift."

"I love you too, Samuel John." Tears began to swell up in her eyes, as she turned away from him. Sara Jane began to call Cindy and Daisy to supper as Joseph Levi, Jacob and Levi came into the back porch. The men took their boots off and hung their straw hats on the rack.

Betty Anne was surprised at how grown up these young men were.

She began thinking to herself, "The girls are so precious with their hair pulled back into a bun. They are young Amish girl's now. The horrible past they endured is erased from their memory forever." The family sat down at the table with Betty Anne sitting between Cindy and Daisy. They bowed their heads as Levi said the silent prayer. Levi fills each plate and passes it to Sara Jane. She hands each one of the younger children their plates. She filled their glasses with milk and offered Betty Anne a cup of tea.

She had made a delicious dinner with roast chicken boiled potatoes and green beans from her garden; along with homemade biscuits. The kids ate everything on their plates except Joseph Levi; he only ate the vegetables. Sara Jane said. "He loves animals so much he can't eat the meat. From the time he was just a little boy he has wanted to be a veterinarian." Levi, spoke up and said. "I am disappointed that you don't want to be a blacksmith, Joseph Levi."

"I know dad, but I have always had a dream of becoming a veterinarian. I can still help you out from time to time if you need me."

Chapter Five

Samuel John had been in the hospital all summer and fall, and now it was too cold to go outside. He longed to go and play in the snow; and go back to school. When he woke up one morning, he called his mama, but she had gone out to collect eggs at the barn. He decided to get up and look for her. He moved one leg at a time and managed to walk toward the kitchen. His mama was coming in off the back porch when she saw him. She was surprised and angry with him for not waiting for her to help him.

Samuel John's feelings were hurt, and tears started rolling down his face. "When I woke up, you were gone. I missed you, mama. I thought you would be proud of me for walking."

She gave him a big hug. "I am proud of you but afraid you will get hurt." He wanted her to let him walk on his own. Later that day while the girls were at school, she pulled Samuel John up out of his wheelchair. He stood up by himself and put one foot at a time forward, then the other foot. Sara Jane was overcome with happiness for him. "I am so proud of you, but you need to lie down now and rest for a while. I don't want you to overdo it today."

She knew if he could practice walking once a day like that, it was only a matter of time before he would be walking. Sara Jane was concerned because he had a limp when he walked. She said a silent prayer for Samuel John, *"Please Lord, let my son be able to walk again and be a healthy boy; God bless him and give him the strength he needs to walk."* She thought of Joseph Levi and what he had to go through; he would be on medication for the rest of his life.

She asked God, *"Why have both of my boys had to go through such tragic events?"*

Levi was so proud of Samuel John that he decided that he would make him a cane to assist him when he walked. The boy would be completely out of breath just walking across the room. At least he would have something he could hold on to and feel more secure. He went out into the woods and found a small pine tree that he could cut down. He dragged it to the barn and began to saw the wood. He sawed it till he had just the right length and height. He rubbed oil on it until it was smooth and then decided he would carve Samuel John's initials into the side of it.

Whenever Samuel John walked, he would get tired; so his mama would only let him walk a little each day. Most of the time he would sit in his wheelchair and read books or play a game with the girls. When Levi finished the cane, he brought it into the house to give to Samuel John. The boy was so excited to get it. "Thank you father for the cane, it's going to help me walk better; I just know it." The following day, Sara Jane helped him up. "Samuel John use the cane when you walk, you will be able to pull yourself out of the chair and walk across the room." The cane made Samuel John feel more safe and secure.

The days were getting longer and warmer as spring began to come to Ruby Hope Valley.

Flowers of all kinds began to pop up out of the ground. The air was breezy and refreshing. The Amish men and boys were out in the fields getting the ground ready for planting season. They would plant corn, green beans, and pumpkins. The pumpkins would be ready by fall for the market. Sara Jane had started planting her flowers against the side of the house. Samuel John's legs were still very weak, so he would sit on the front porch in the wheelchair most of the day.

Sometimes he would use the cane and walk around the yard.

One afternoon, while walking with his cane, he decided to walk down to the barn. His dad was in the barn working as he approached. "Dad, I want to try and ride my horse again; may I?" Levi was against it as he said, "No boy that's not a good idea now." Samuel John was disappointed but knew his dad was right. He asked his mother one day. "When can I start back to school, mama?" "I'm not sure Samuel John; we will need to talk to Doctor Huddleston and see what he says." He had always been an active boy; now all he could do was sit on the front porch. He had gotten so used to the cane; he was afraid he may never walk without it again.

Sometimes when he felt lonely or depressed, he would take the compass that Betty Anne had given him out of his pocket and look at it. He would remember what Betty Anne said to him, "It will always guide you home." He put it back in his pocket and decided he would carry it wherever he went.

Chapter Six

Betty Anne had been volunteering at the state foster institute for almost twenty years now and had helped many children get adopted. She loved being around the children and worked tirelessly to find homes for as many as she could. She decided it was time for her to slow down a little when the foster home called her. "Mrs. Miller there's a young boy about four years old and his little sister, who looks to be about two. They have just arrived and seem to be victims of child abuse. We need your help." She thought to herself, "I can't let these kids go through this alone; I need to help them."

She drove over to the foster home to meet the two children. Johnny was four and Katy was two. Her heart broke when she saw them. They had bruises all over their arms and legs.

Betty Anne was outraged when she saw this and struggled to hide the tears rolling down her face.

She took them into her arms and hugged them. They seemed to be scared at first, but Betty Anne had such a sweet loving face that they were not afraid anymore. She had gained a lot of weight in her old age, but was still just as pleasant and warm as always.

She thought about Jacob, Cindy, and Daisy and how abused they had been before coming to the foster home. The family had been through so much over the years but were blessed when the three kids came to live with them. First Joseph Levi and his kidney transplant and then Samuel John and the accident he had with his horse, Abby. "What could happen to them next?"

She didn't want to think about that and started to pray. *"Dear Lord, please keep Sara Jane and Levi's family safe and well."*

Betty Anne went back to the foster home the following day. When she arrived, the two children were taking a nap, so she decided this was an excellent time to speak to the supervisor; Becky White. "Becky, where were the children found?"

"They were found walking down the road around midnight. A nurse at the hospital spotted them as she was getting off duty. She was walking to her car when she noticed them. She approached them and asked them where they lived, but they were too scared to speak. She immediately took them to the police department.

The police officer tried to talk to the kids, but neither one of them would say anything.

They were so young and had no idea where their home was. The Policeman brought the kids here for us to take care of until they could find out whom they belonged to." Betty Anne couldn't believe this and remembered another case of abuse she had to deal with, a few years before. "I can't believe how people treat their children. It's a miracle and a blessing to have children in the first place. I wish there was something I could do about all this abuse."

When the children came downstairs, she asked them if they were hungry. "I'll take you to the dining room and get you something to eat." The kitchen attendant made them peanut butter and jelly sandwiches and poured them a glass of milk. Betty Anne sat with them while they ate.

After they had eaten dinner, she gave them both another big hug and took them back upstairs to lie down. She tucked them in their beds and sat there beside them for a while. She spoke out loud to herself, "how anyone could treat little innocent children like this is beyond me." Tears started to roll down her face as she watched them silently sleep.

They seemed so tired and broken. The following day, she was up bright and early. She got a call from Sadie and told her about the children that just came into the foster home. "I am going to see if I can find a good home for them."

"You are a miracle worker, mother, and I know if anyone can find them a home, it's my mother." Sadie had called to tell Betty Anne she and Emily Grace were coming for a short visit. "I am so excited about your visit. When are you coming?"

"I have a few vacation days I need to take, so I decided to come for a visit. We will be arriving next Friday afternoon."

In the meantime, the police officer stopped by the home to see Becky White and fill her in on the information they had on the two children. Betty Anne arrived at the orphanage just in time to hear what he had to say. John Wilson said. "The mother and father were drinking and doing drugs. They live in the Oak Forrest area, which is a small suburb of Ruby Hope. They seem to have a decent home. But the kids' father has been laid off from his job and apparently, the parents neglected the children while drinking.

Their grandmother called The Department of Family and Children Services several times about the abuse but as far as she knows, they never responded. She wanted to take the children and keep them herself. Do you think the children could stay at the home until their mother and father go to court. The grandmother will be coming by to see them from time to time. The parents have a restraining order against them, so, they aren't allowed to come near the children."

Betty Anne was in complete shock at what the policeman told them. She spoke up and said just what she was thinking. "I can't believe any parent would burn their little child with a cigarette or anything for that matter. And to knock them around whenever they felt like it. How horrible can these people be?"

"The Children can stay here as long as they need to. They will be well taken care of Sergeant." Replied Becky White. Betty Ann spoke up, "The children need a good home: with people who won't abuse them."

Chapter Seven

Betty Anne needed to go home and get ready for Sadie and Emily Grace's visit, but she hated to leave these little children. She just felt the need to take care of them. Mrs. White told her to go ahead and go home. "I will take good care of the kids; and make sure no harm comes to them." Betty Anne decided she would leave and come back the next day. She needed to clean the house and bake something good for her daughter. She was so happy they were coming to visit and could hardly wait to see them.

Spring had finally arrived in Ruby Hope, but the weather was still a little cool. There was still snow on the ground. That's the way it was every year thought, Betty Anne. The following morning, Betty Anne got up early and got dressed; and ate a small breakfast Her neighbor Barbara knocked on the front door as she was getting ready to leave. "Come on in Barbara, I want to tell you about the two small children that came to the foster home the other day. I was just about to head over there to visit them."

She told her about how they had been abused by their parents, and the grandmother was hoping to get them and raise them. Barbara said. "Would you mind if I went with you today?"

"I've been thinking about becoming a volunteer and would love to volunteer at the foster home."

"Of course, Barbara, I'm so happy you want to volunteer. Come on, let's get started."

As they drove over to the foster home, Betty Anne told Barbara about Sadie and Emily Grace's visit on Friday. "Would you like to come over and have dinner one evening?"

Barbara was delighted and replied. "I would love to."

As they pulled into the parking lot, she noticed a police car parked in front of the home.

She wondered if something had happened to the kids and could hardly wait to go inside the building. When they walked in the door, they saw John Wilson, the police officer. Betty Anne asked. "Has something happened?"

"No, it isn't anything to worry about, the kids are fine.

Sergeant Wilson has just stopped by to check on them." He said. "I had a hard time going to sleep last night, all I could think of was those two little kids."

The following Friday Sadie and Emily Grace arrived in Ruby Hope. Betty Anne said. "Sadie, why did you drive all this way instead of taking the train?"

"I wanted to see how long it would take me to drive here. I think I will come by train next time."

"I think that's a good idea." Emily Grace was four years old and a beautiful little girl with dark brown hair and big brown eyes. She had a smile that would light up a room. Betty Anne was so proud of her granddaughter. While enjoying a delicious dinner that evening, they had a nice visit. Betty Anne had even baked an apple pie. It was almost as good as Sara Jane's; almost.

The Best of Amish Cooking Written by Phyllis Pellman Good'

The German settlers brought their love of pastries to Pennsylvania. What they learned from their English neighbors in the New World was how to fashion that fondness into pies. And pies have been on Amish menus ever since.

Recipe for Amish Apple Pie:

6 cups apples, peeled and sliced
½ - ¼ cup sugar (depending upon the flavor of the apples)
2 Tbsp. flour
¾ tsp. cinnamon
2 Tbsp. lemon juice
1 9" unbaked pie shell and top crust

After dinner, Sadie put Emily Grace to bed. They sat in the kitchen while they drank coffee and talked. Betty Anne began to tell Sadie about the two little-abused kids that just came into foster care. "I am so concerned about them and wonder what I should do?"

Sadie said. "You need to be patient and see what happens with the parents in court. Just be a friend, and show them someone cares about them. I would love to ride out to the farm and see Sara Jane and the family. I have been thinking about Samuel John a lot and wanted to see how he is coming along."

Saturday morning Sadie, Betty Anne, and Emily Grace got up early; dressed and ate breakfast. Betty Anne made a special breakfast of pancakes and sausage patties. Sadie said. "Mother, those pancakes were the best I have ever eaten. Could you give me the recipe?"

"Of course, it's one of Sara Jane's. She is a wonderful cook, all those Amish women are good cooks. They know just how to spice up a casserole and their baking is superb. See all these pounds I have put on, it's from eating all that Amish food Sara Jane cooks. She is constantly baking pies and cakes. I am surprised she doesn't weigh two hundred pounds."

As they drove out to the Amish Community, the landscape was so lovely. The grass was starting to turn green and flowers were popping up out of the ground along the fence line. They could see the Amish men and their sons bailing hay and planting seeds. The cows were laying down in the pastures, and the horses were in the fields eating grass. "Mother, how have you been feeling lately? Have you had any problems with your heart?"

Betty Anne was reluctant to talk about her health; she didn't want Sadie to worry about her. "I'm doing just fine Sadie." You stay at the foster home too much and worry about those kids all the time. I know you love being there and working with the kids, but mother you have got to slow down."

"I can't help but worry about them and want to help them if I can." Sadie finally decided this was what made her mother happy, but she still worried about her. "Please try to get as much rest as you can."

Chapter Eight

As they were driving up the dirt road that leads to Sara Jane and Levi's farm, they could see Levi and the two boys out in the fields planting seeds. Samuel John was sitting on the front porch in his wheelchair. Cindy and Daisy were playing with their dolls alongside him. Emily Grace was excited to see the girls and wanted to play with them. Betty Anne hugged Samuel John and asked him, "How are you feeling today, Samuel?" "I'm ok but wish I could get out of this chair."

"Do you still have the compass I gave you?" He pulled it out of his pants pocket and showed it to her. "Remember it will always show you the way home if you ever get lost."

Sara Jane invited them in for a cup of tea and a slice of fresh bread. She had just taken it out of the wood stove. It smelled so delicious they couldn't wait to taste it. They sat down at the kitchen table as Betty Anne said. "How is Samuel John doing?" Sara Jane said. "He is walking with a cane from time to time. His legs are still weak, and the doctor says it's going to take a long time for them to get stronger." Betty Anne thought to herself, "the boy has been home for a while now and should be showing some improvement in his legs." Sara Jane said. "I am really worried that he may never be able to walk on his own again."

"Now, Sara Jane, it's not like you to give up hope. Hope and faith in the future are all we have. Your faith in God will get you through this. I truly believe Samuel John is going to walk on his own one day." Betty Anne and Sadie gave Sara Jane a big hug and huddled together as they said a prayer with her. The girls were having a good time playing jumping jacks on the front porch. They had Samuel John involved, and he seemed to be having a good time with them. Sara Jane had made the girls some new Amish dolls and had an extra one, so she asked Sadie, "Do you mind if Emily Grace has an Amish doll?" Sadie said. "I don't have any objections to her having the doll." Sara Jane gave one of the dolls to the child. Emily Grace was so excited to get the little Amish doll, she smiled as if to say, "thank you." She said. "Mommy, I love this baby doll, and I'm going to name her Sammy." Sadie said. "But that's a boy's name?" She just kept saying I want to call my doll Sammy, mommy. The three women laughed and laughed at Emily Grace.

After a while, it was time for them to leave, Betty Anne wanted to get back to Ruby Hope before dark. They all hugged and said their goodbyes, as always, she had tears starting to roll down her face. She loved this family so much, and it hurt her every time she had to leave them. They had shared so much through the years, and she was always worried about what might happen next. Sara Jane and Levi had been through so much with their two sons but still found it in their hearts to open their home to three more children. *She said a silent prayer for this family and prayed for God to bless them and keep them all safe and well.*

Sadie knew how much her mother loved this family and thought it was a good thing they were in her life. Even though she lived a long way from her, she knew there were people to look after her and love her. "Sadie, would you like to go to the foster home tomorrow and see the children?"

"Oh yes, I'd love to go and see where my mother spends most of her time."

"Maybe you can find another nice Amish family who will take the two children in?"

"I've thought about that, but the police are investigating the situation, and we must wait and see what the court's decision is going to be."

The following day they rode over to the foster home to see the children. When they arrived, the policeman was there talking with Becky White. "Betty Anne, the court has decided the children should stay here until we can find them a foster home. It's in their best interest because of their parent's abusive behavior. Their grandmother is too old and in bad health, so the court is against her taking the children in."

"I'm happy for the children and think the court has made the right decision for them. Is it ok if I introduce Sadie to the kids?" Becky asked one of the older girls to go and bring them down to her office.

Johnny and Katy came down the stairs; as Betty Anne hardly recognized them. Their bruises and cigarette burns had almost disappeared, and they wore clean clothes. When Emily Grace saw the little girl she handed her the Amish doll and told her she could keep it. Katy was only two years old and took the doll and held it to her chest. The child smiled at her and Sadie was so proud of Emily Grace. "That is so sweet of you, Emily Grace, to give up your little doll."

Becky White said. "The kids will have to stay with us for a while before they can go to a foster home."

"Betty Anne smiled and said. "I'll start looking for a home right away."

She knew these two kids needed to be in a safe and loving environment. She had come to feel like her goal in life was to help as many children as she could. On the drive home, she told Sadie about Barbara wanting to become a volunteer at the foster home. "I'm so happy to have her help." Sadie was so proud of her mother and gave her a big hug. "All these kids are lucky to have such a sweet loving woman here that cares about them."

Chapter Nine

The following day, Sadie and Emily Grace left to go back home to New York. Betty Anne was heartbroken to see them leave. She loved having them come to visit her. She went out to work in her garden after they left. It made her forget her problems and gave her a feeling of serenity. She felt peaceful and calm while working with her flowers. After a while she decided to go inside and lay down for a while; she was so tired she could hardly make it into the house.

After resting for a while, she decided she wanted to go shopping and buy the two children some new clothes. She couldn't stop thinking about them. She thought to herself, "If only I was a younger woman; I would take them in myself." She went into Ruby Hope and found a little shop that had a lot of children's clothes. She decided on a pair of overalls for Johnny with a cute cowboy shirt to go with them. She also bought him a new pair of sneakers to wear. She had to guess on his shoe size but felt confident she had gotten the right ones. She bought Katy two adorable dresses and a pair of sneakers too As the days and weeks passed, the children became accustomed to their new environment and started to feel comfortable around the other children. Betty Anne and Barbara would volunteer their time two or three days a week. Johnny and Katy loved Betty Anne and couldn't wait to see her. She adored these two kids and was determined to find them a good foster home. Barbara began to love going out to the home and decided she would become an advocate for the kids.

Barbara decided she was going to start speaking out for the children; and helping the local foster care home raise money. She said. "They need money desperately to run the facility." Betty Anne spoke up and said. "The state of Pennsylvania funds the foster care system, but it just isn't enough. The children need clothes and shoes; and they never have enough beds.

We need to get a campaign started and get the Ruby Hope media involved. Maybe have them advertise in the newspaper about the kids. The signs in the windows of the stores in town aren't doing enough." The two women would set in motion a campaign like no other.

The weeks that followed were hectic for Betty Anne and Barbara. They had set out on a journey to find these kids new foster homes or get them adopted. Betty Anne said. "Barbara, there isn't enough money from the state to provide the crucial things these kids need. Like Johnny and Katy need therapy to help them overcome their fears. It would seem like the state would provide a good therapist for them; but there aren't enough good ones around. So, it's hard for the ones that are twelve or older to adjust. They have trust problems too."

They worked together to get the community of Ruby Hope and surrounding areas to be aware of the needs the foster care system had. Barbara went to the local newspaper in Ruby Hope and told them all about the children that needed foster homes or to be adopted. She said.

"There are just too many kids and not enough people helping to take care of them. The public needs to know about the abused ones and the need for clothes and beds. They should know that the state isn't providing for the kids the way they should."

By the time Barbara was through talking to the newspaper lady, she had her in tears.

Janet Barns was a good reporter, but she had never thought to investigate the foster care system before. She understood the concerns Barbara had and told her she was going to check into these problems. Janet decided that she would take a trip out to the local foster care facility and see for herself. She wanted to get a firsthand look at the kids and talk to the administrator that ran the home.

"I am so proud of you Barbara for going to the newspaper, and I hope they insert everything you told them in their paper. I want the people of Ruby Hope and the Amish Community to be aware of the situation. Why don't we rent a billboard too, and have a large advertisement describing the kids on it. And we could put some of the kid's pictures on there too, so people could see them."

"Yes, and everyone will surely be aware once they see the billboard." Replied Barbara. Betty Anne and Barbara were both tired and decided they had done enough for one day and decided to go home.

After Janet Barns visited the foster home, she wrote a nice column about the kids she met there. She had seen firsthand the needs of the home. She stressed about how over-crowded they were and how much they needed people to help give these kids a good foster home. It brought a lot of attention to the home and Becky White was stunned at the response she had received. She was getting calls from families wanting to foster some of the children or adopt them. She even received a call from the Mayor. He told her he was going to check into the situation and try to get them more money to run the facility.

Donations began to flow into the home and Betty Anne and Barbara were amazed at how generous the people of their town were. Levi and Sara Jane heard what Betty Anne and Barbara had done for the foster home. Sara Jane said to Betty Anne. "We are proud of you and Barbara.

Levi and I have decided to talk with other Amish families in our community. We want to see if there is anyone interested in fostering or adopting a child." The Amish folks knew all about Levi and Sara Jane adopting the three orphans' years before. She was excited when her people said they would consider adopting.

Chapter Ten

Summer had come and gone so fast that Betty Anne could hardly believe it. She worked all summer tirelessly for the foster home. She was talking to Sadie on the phone one night and told her what had been going on. "Johnny and Katy have been fostered by a couple from Ruby Hope. Their mother and father must follow the rules of the court to try and get their lives back together. They're both in therapy and going to AA meetings now. They told the court they would do anything to get their two children back. I think when the father lost his job, they couldn't pay their bills; things got out of hand.

The newspaper article and the two billboards had done what the two women wanted. It brought attention to the kids in the foster care system. "Sadie, the state gave the home more money too so they can get the things they need to run the facility as it should be." Sadie was in awe of all this and said. "I am so proud of you and Barbara for bringing the awareness the town needed to the foster home situation. You two ladies are exceptional and should receive an award for all you do."

Becky White couldn't thank Betty Anne and Barbara enough. Most of the small children were adopted out and several of the older ones placed in foster homes. Betty Anne made sure they were decent homes and did her own investigating into their backgrounds. She couldn't stand the thought of any of these kids being abused.

It was fall of the year and the days were getting cooler. The leaves on the trees were already turning brown, red and gold. Trees that lined the streets of downtown Ruby Hope were beautiful this time of year. The farmers were bringing their pumpkins into town by the truck loads; to sell to the local markets. The stores in town had pumpkins lined up in front of their buildings, and the Churchyards were scattered with all shapes and sizes of pumpkins for sale.

Betty Anne loved this time of year and wanted to take a drive out to see Sara Jane and the family. She wanted to check on Joseph Levi and Samuel John to see how they were doing. She had not been out to visit them for about a month. She had been busy working with the kids at the foster home, and it seemed to take up a lot of her time. She wanted to tell Sara Jane all about her quest to save these kids during the summer and check on Jacob, Cindy and Daisy as well. She knew Sara Jane would be interested because of her work with the kids in the past.

She loved the drive to the farm; the landscape was so beautiful. The Amish people were always working on their land and you never saw any trash or litter anywhere. The fields and rolling hills was always green with colorful flowers. It also gave her time to think and reminisce about her life. She thought of Danny and Sadie as tears swelled up in her eyes.

She got her daughter back but lost her son; she knew the heartache she felt would never go away. It was so painful to think of Danny, but he was always on her mind and in her heart.

As she approached the farm, she saw Levi, Joseph Levi and Jacob loading up the wagon with the pumpkins they had grown. They were getting ready to take them into town. That was one of the first things Sara Jane wanted Levi to plant when they moved to the farm. They waved to her and continued working. She was amazed at how grown the boys looked and so handsome too. Betty Anne wondered if the young men had started their courting yet. Sara Jane saw her coming and was happy to see her.

She invited her to come into the kitchen and sit down. "Samuel John is taking a nap now."

"How is the boy doing these days?" Sara Jane said. "His legs don't seem to be getting any stronger and we are very concerned about him. He seems to be depressed all the time and doesn't have much interest in doing anything. He uses the cane Levi made but he gets frustrated with it."

"How is Cindy and Daisy doing these days?"

Sara Jane poured them a cup of tea and offered her slice of bread. "They are still at school and I am sorry you missed seeing them. The girls have been a life saver for Samuel John. They read to him and play games with him as if they wanted to protect him and take care of him all the time. When they are not here, he just sits and looks out the door or takes a nap. He has no interest in anything, and we are worried sick about him."

Betty Anne was concerned about Samuel John and wished she could do something to help him. Betty Anne began to tell Sara Jane about the foster home. "The home has become so crowded that Barbara and I started a campaign to help the kids get new homes and more money to run on." Sara Jane was so proud of her and said. "I heard about the work you and Barbara have done. I have spoken to several of the Amish families to see if they would foster some of the children."

"The response has been overwhelming from the article in the newspaper and the billboards. I just know the children will find new homes." Replied Betty Anne.

The two women had a nice visit as always. "I need to be on my way home." As she drove home she couldn't stop thinking about Samuel John and wondered what she could do to help him. She began to think. "There seems to be a new project for me just around the corner; I know it will be a difficult one for sure." Betty Anne would need to think about this for a while but knew in her heart she would come up with something to help him. She said a a silent prayer for Samuel John and asked *God to guide her and help her to find a way to help this child.*

The weather began to get colder as Thanksgiving approached. Betty Anne would join the family once again this year. She had spent the last several years with the family and could hardly wait to be with them on this special holiday. She went shopping and bought a big turkey, fruit, flour and sugar for Sara Jane. She thought as much as she baked, she could use some supplies.

Levi had always been against Betty Anne's gift giving; it wasn't the Amish way. He knew how much she meant to Sara Jane and the family, so it was useless to bring it up. Each time she brought gifts to them, he would overlook it.

Chapter Eleven

Sara Jane had invited her dad and her brother John to spend Thanksgiving with them once again, this year. Mark said the silent prayer as he always did and then looked around the table and smiled. "Just look at all these children, I am grateful for all of you. A house is not a home without children." Sara Jane and Levi just looked at him and then looked at all the kids and said. "Amen dad."

Sara Jane's brother, John, never married; he could never get over Rose. He said to Sara Jane. "Rose was the only girl for me and now it is too late. Rose is married now to a local Amish boy from Lancaster. I'm just not interested in meeting any other girls in the community. That's why I never go to the singings or any gatherings the young folks have." He worked his little farm and helped his dad on his. Sara Jane was determined to find him a wife.

She knew several young women in their district that had not married, but John didn't seem interested.

Joseph Levi and Jacob had become courting age, so they started going to the singing at Mr. Wilkerson's old barn. All the young folks would meet there on Saturday nights. They would choose a girl they liked and talk with her for a while, then ask her if she would like to go riding around in their buggy. Levi had told the two boys, "Y'all will have to share the buggy."

Joseph Levi and Jacob didn't like that idea, but decided they would switch off each Sunday they took a girl riding around. One weekend Jacob would have the buggy and the next Joseph Levi would have it. This seemed to work out ok for the two boys.

Joseph Levi was feeling good and taking his medicine every day. He got it in his head if he was old enough to go courting, then he was old enough to go away to school. He never gave up on the idea of becoming a veterinarian. He decided he would go and ask Jim Peterson, the local veterinarian if he could help in his clinic. He was fifteen years old and wanted to get experience with a real veterinarian. "I would be happy to have you work here part-time. I need someone to help around here. Since you are interested in becoming a veterinarian, I will even let you watch me operate on the animals. Then you will have experience."

Joseph Levi was so excited that he could hardly wait to ask his dad if he could work at the clinic. "I will do all my chores in the morning and then go to the clinic in the afternoon, dad." Levi wasn't so sure he liked the idea of him working in the clinic. "You will need to talk with the Bishop first and see what he thinks about this. If it's ok with him, then I will agree to let you go." Levi knew that Joseph Levi had wanted to be a veterinarian his whole life and it seemed nothing was going to change his mind.

The next day, Joseph Levi went to see the Bishop to ask his permission to help in the clinic. Everyone in the Amish Community knew about Joseph Levi's love of animals and his dream of becoming a vet. It wasn't against their rules to leave the district to go to school, but with only an eighth-grade education made it difficult to get into a college. Joseph Levi desperately wanted permission to work in the clinic. The Bishop said. "As long as you don't except money, there is no reason why you can't help out there." The boy was elated, and couldn't wait to tell the family. They agreed to let him go and help in the clinic, but still hoped he would change his mind. The boy didn't have any intentions of changing his mind.

The following week, Joseph Levi got up early and went to the barn to do his chores.

He cleaned all the horse stalls, fed the horses, and laid down fresh straw. He fed the pigs, chickens, and cows and swept out the barn stalls. When Levi entered the barn, he was amazed at what the boy had done. He patted the boy on his back and said. "You have done a good job; now let's go in the house and eat breakfast." Sara Jane had breakfast ready on the table when Joseph Levi and his dad came in the house. Joseph Levi was so anxious to get started he wasn't hungry.

Chapter Twelve

The animal clinic was just a couple of miles from the farm. Joseph Levi knew it was going to snow soon as it always did this time of year. Jacob said. "Come on, I"ll take you in the carriage and pick you up around 4:00 this afternoon." The two boys climbed into the carriage and headed down the road to the veterinarian clinic. Jim Peterson was happy to see Joseph Levi and told him what needed to be done. The boy put on an apron he gave him to wear and started checking out all the dogs in their cages.

He came across one dog they called Maggie and decided he would walk her first.

He asked Jim about her and if she belonged to anyone. "Just so happens Maggie was found on the side of the road with a hurt leg. Are you interested in taking Maggie home with you?"

"I really like the dog Jim, but I need to check with mama and dad first."

In the meantime, he took each dog out in the back of the building and walked them around for a while. Then he bathed three of the dogs. After he had finished, he began cleaning the cages. Every time he passed Maggie's cage, he stopped to pet her. She was a sweet dog and loved the attention she was getting from him. "Joseph Levi, you are doing a great job, I don't know how I ever got along without you."

Joseph Levi loved being around all the cats and dogs and knew in his heart no matter what, this was what he wanted to do for the rest of his life. It was almost 4:00 and Jacob would be there to pick him up. He went over to Maggie's cage and petted her. "I'll see you tomorrow girl." On the ride home, he told Jacob about Maggie. "She sounds like a pretty nice dog, why don't you ask dad if you can bring her home?"

"I wanted to wait a while before mentioning it to dad. In the meantime, I want to get as close to the dog as I can."

The boy continued to get up early every morning and do his chores in the barn. Levi knew in his heart that his son loved working at the animal clinic; and he had his heart set on becoming a veterinarian. Joseph Levi had been working at the animal clinic for several weeks and was so fond of Maggie. He hated leaving her in that cage every day but knew he needed to ask his dad if he could bring her home. Jim said. "I'm going to close the clinic the day before Christmas and reopen the day after New Year's. Do you want to take Maggie home because you can have her if you want her."

I need someone to come by every day we're closed to give the animal's food and water.

And I wanted to see if you are willing to do it if I pay you."

"I can't accept any money for the job, Jim, but I would like to take care of the animals." Jim gave him the key to the clinic and said. "You need to call me on the phone in the clinic if you have any problems."

It was 4:00 and time for Jacob to pick him up. The boy was excited about the dog and decided he would ask his dad if he could bring her home to the farm. After arriving home, he went to the barn to talk to his dad. Levi was busy now, but he asked him anyway. "What's on your mind son?"

"Dad, Jim asked if I would take care of the animals during the holidays." Dad said. "You know the weather is going to be bad and you might have a hard time getting there every day."

The snow had begun to fall hard, and the roads were treacherous with debris and limbs. Joseph Levi thought, "I'm worried about the weather but I know I have to get to the clinic somehow."

"Jacob would you like to go with me to the animal clinic and help me feed the dogs and cats during the holidays?" Jacob was excited about going. He knew they would need to take the enclosed carriage because it was so cold. The horses could barely pull the carriage, with all the snow and ice on the ground.

After finally arriving at the clinic, they fed the animals and gave them fresh water. They walked some of the dogs around inside the clinic; to give them a little exercise. Joseph Levi could hardly wait for Jacob to meet Maggie. She was a brown, medium size Shih Tzu with big brown eyes. Jacob fell in love with Maggie. "Joseph Levi, you need to go ahead and ask dad if you can bring her home."

"I was planning to ask him, but he has been so busy lately."

The following day, Joseph Levi went to the barn early that morning to get his chores done. Dad and Jacob came in shortly after him talking about how cold it was. He decided while Jacob was there; he would ask his dad about Maggie. "Dad, there is a dog at the clinic that I would love to bring home to the farm, her name is Maggie, and she is a real sweet dog dad. She needs a good home." Dad responded to him, "I don't want any little puppies running around the place."

"All that has been taken care of. She is a sweet and loving dog, and and it may help Samuel John too, dad." He made his case, now it was time for dad to respond.

Levi took his straw hat off, scratched his head, stood there as if he was thinking about all of this.Levi finally spoke, "Alright then, but you will have to be responsible for the dog and make sure she has been fed every day. If you can do that, you can bring her home." The two boys were so excited and started running around and around. "Now boys calm down and get your chores done." After they had done all their chores, they ran into the house and told Sara Jane that they were getting a dog called Maggie May. Samuel John and the girls were excited and started laughing, jumping up and down and screaming.

The weather outside the farmhouse was hovering around 28 degrees, but you would never know it from the sound inside. They were having a wonderful Christmas that year. Sara Jane asked Betty Anne, her father and her brother John to join them for dinner; as she always did for the holidays. She had baked a roast chicken with gravy, mashed potatoes, corn on the cob and green beans. She had canned all the vegetables last summer and had them stored in the cellar.

These Amish children were having so much fun playing games and enjoying the warmth from the fireplace; they never noticed how cold it was outside.

Chapter Thirteen

After the holidays were over, Joseph Levi brought Maggie May home from the animal clinic. Jim Peterson said. "I am happy Maggie May is getting a good home."

"Jim, she is going to be the queen bee of our farm. I think Maggie is going to help Samuel John, too. He needs something in his life to care for." Joseph Levi continued to work at the clinic in the afternoons.

He loved taking care of the animals and was very good with them. Jim said to him. "One day this week I am going to operate on one of the little dogs; it needs a tumor removed. Would you like to assist with the operation?"

Joseph Levi was so excited and said. "I would love to Jim." The boy stood by the operating table and assisted Jim with the instruments he needed. Jim said. "Joseph Levi, you have a true calling, and you should pursue it one day."

"I have always wanted to go away to school and learn to be a veterinarian. But being Amish keeps me from pursuing my dream." Jim knew the rules of the Amish people because he had lived among them for several years. In fact, it took him a long time to get the community to accept him as their veterinarian.

The children were so excited when they saw Maggie May. Joseph Levi said. "Y'all need to calm down and stop screaming and running around, because you are scaring the dog. It makes her nervous. She's not used to kids yet." Cindy and Daisy spoke softly to her after that. The family came to love Maggie as she became a part of their family. She slept with Joseph Levi and Jacob every night but when morning rolled around, she would go looking for Cindy and Daisy.

Maggie

It was a lovely spring day when Levi decided to ride into town. He needed to stop by the local hardware store and pick up a few items for the shop. Jim Peterson, the local veterinarian, saw Levi and decided to speak to him about Joseph Levi. "Hi Mr. Click, I'm Jim Peterson, I've been wanting to speak to you about your son. Joseph Levi is one of the smartest young men I have ever met before. He was a life saver for me over the holidays. Mr. Click, you should be so proud of the boy, he is going to make a great veterinarian one day."

On the way home, Levi began to reminisce about Joseph Levi. He had always wanted to be a veterinarian and it didn't look like anything was going to change his mind. With only an eighth-grade education it was almost impossible. What to do was clearly on his mind and he knew he needed to talk to his son. The sooner the better.

Jacob Hackle, Mennonite resident of Lancaster County, home of the Amish answered the question:

The Amish formal educational experience ends at the end of eight grade. As they don't have a 12th grade education and often don't have a GED getting into a college would be rather hard.

Instead of more formal education, further learning is done in a hands-on manner either working on a farm, construction crew, or small manufacturing shop (machine parts, cabinetry, etc.)

Joseph Levi continued to help at the animal clinic. Jim Peterson taught him as much as he could about being a veterinarian. He let him assist him on all operations and procedures until Joseph Levi felt he could do them himself. After working for over two years at the animal clinic, Jim said to him. "It's going to be difficult for you to go to college.

I have a suggestion. You could take some correspondent courses and get your certificate to practice."

This interested Joseph Levi and he thought he would talk to his father about it.

Amish America Newsletter:

Some Amish, especially businesspeople, may take supplemental courses, such as correspondence Classes', or may attend seminars or classes to pick up a skill. The emphasis is on Practicality and Usefulness. Amish do not see education as evil or dangerous.

One evening after dinner, Levi was sitting in the living room reading the local Amish paper, when Joseph Levi entered the room. Joseph Levi said. "Can I talk to you about something?" The boy was seventeen by now and old enough to make up his own mind about things. "Dad, Jim Peterson told me I could take some correspondent courses. I already have hands on experience since working at the animal clinic. All I need to do to get the certificate is to take these courses. They would come in the mail and it would be just like going to school again."

"If the Bishop says it's ok, then you can go ahead and take the courses."

"Oh dad, thank you for doing this for me."

Chapter Fourteen

Over the past two years, Samuel John had gotten his strength back in his legs. He still had to use a cane but could get around well. He was fourteen years old now and wanted to ride his horse, Abby, but Levi forbids him to ride her. Levi gave him the job of taking care of the horses every day. Samuel John's duties were to brush the horses down each day and give them fresh oaks and water. He could walk them around for exercise in the big field, but he couldn't ride them. He was so disappointed but even he knew his dad was right and obeyed him no matter what.

Jacob had been going to the singing on Saturday nights and met a girl by the name of Grace Fisher. He said. "Joseph Levi, I want to marry Grace and have a small farm of my own.

She knows I'm adopted but doesn't mind because I have been baptized into the Amish church. I am eighteen now and I want to settle down and start a family of my own. I want to be the best father in the world because I never knew my real father. Levi is the greatest man I have ever known and I want to be just like him."

Joseph Levi said. "I am so happy for you and I want to help you find a small farm. I'm sure, dad knows of one. We will ask him." Joseph Levi was only interested in getting his certificate to practice at the animal clinic, so he stopped going to the singings and wasn't interested in any one girl. He thought maybe one day he would find someone, but for now his heart was set on becoming a vet. Jim Peterson said to Joseph Levi. "You can continue to work with me and maybe one day become my partner." Joseph Levi was excited about that prospect and told Jacob all about it.

It was a beautiful spring afternoon, when Levi showed up at the animal clinic. Joseph Levi was surprised to see him there. Levi said to him. "I spoke with the Bishop and was given permission for you to start taking the courses." He knew how anxious Joseph Levi was, so he wanted to tell him right away. Joseph Levi was excited and told Jim the good news. Jim said to Levi. "Well it looks like I'm going to have a new partner."

That evening at dinner, the whole family was excited for Joseph Levi and wanted him to tell them all about the courses he was going to be taking. He tried to explain to them, but he could see they were having a hard time understanding. He said joking of course, "just remember to bring all your sick animals to me." They all laughed at him as Levi told them to calm down and eat their dinner. Levi gave Joseph Levi the money to order the course he needed through the mail.

It took about four weeks before the paperwork arrived. In the meantime, Jim had started paying Joseph Levi for working with him. He couldn't believe the amount of hours this boy had put in working at the clinic and felt he should be paid. Joseph Levi didn't want to accept the money, but Jim insisted. After all, he had been working there for over two years without being paid and Jim knew it was time he earned something for all his hard work.

In the meantime, the family was going to have a wedding and Sara Jane needed someone to help her, so she called Betty Anne. Jacob had found a small house with an acre, and decided it would be enough to start with. Grace Fisher was excited about the house and couldn't wait to move into it. Grace was a beautiful girl with nut brown hair and blue eyes. Jacob said. "Every time Grace smiles: her eyes sparkle like stars in a blue sky." Her mother, Martha Fisher, lived just down the road from the Clicks. Martha was a pleasant woman who had red cheeks and a boisterous laugh.

Betty Anne was happy to get a call from Sara Jane. She said she would be delighted to help with Jacob's wedding. The wedding was set for June third and it was May already. Sara Jane sat down with Betty Anne and planned out the food menu. "Most of the food will be prepared by the Amish women in the community, but I'm going to make the wedding cake."

Betty Anne had been to several Amish weddings and knew just what to do. She decided the benches would be good on the side of the house where the shade trees were. They would create a nice breeze for everyone. Sara Jane thought that was a perfect idea.

Jacob and his two sisters were very special to Betty Anne. She had been the one who brought the family together. They were a perfect match for this family, and she wanted to do something special for them. She expressed to Sara Jane, she would like to rent a Canopy cover for the yard.

"The women could put the food tables under it." Sara Jane knew Levi would probably be against it, but she felt sure he would give in eventually. Even after all these years of having a Christian woman around all the time, Levi was still set in his ways. "Yes, that sounds perfect. Thank you for all your help Betty Anne, I know Jacob and Grace will appreciate all you do."

Chapter Fifteen

It was a very hot afternoon in May when Martha Fisher came to visit Sara Jane. Her face was as red as an apple and her voice was so loud; Levi could hear her from out in the barn. She seemed upset as she sat down on the front porch with a fan in her hand. Martha told Sara Jane. "I want to have the wedding in our front yard."

"I have already planned everything, and the wedding is going to be here at the farm." Replied Sara Jane.

"Martha, I can really use your help though; would you like to help with the food?" Martha thought for a minute and said, "Yes, I would love to help." Sara Jane said. "Martha this will take all the work away from you and then you can enjoy the wedding with your daughter." Martha seemed relieved after she said this. Jacob had told his mama he wanted roast chicken, mashed potatoes with gravy, corn on the cobb and green beans. So, Sara Jane was determined to have these things for her special adopted son.

Her garden was full of corn stalks and green beans, she just needed to get them picked. She said. "Martha, there are certain requirements for the food, and I need you to tell the other Amish women. Let them know what I need them to bake for the wedding. I'm going to bake the wedding cake and if you have any special dishes Grace loves, please feel free to bake them. I'm also going to roast a chicken and make mashed potatoes, green beans and corn. My sweet Jacob has asked me to make those for his wedding."

Betty Anne got together with the quilting group ladies and asked them to make some white ribbons for the wedding. She wanted to place them around the trees and the post on the front porch. Sara Jane thought that the ribbons would look beautiful and loved her idea.

The wedding plans were coming along well, and both the woman wanted everything to be special for Jacob.

From the first day he came to the farm with his sister's, Cindy and Daisy, he had been a good child. He was quiet and shy and would always do what he was told. He was afraid if he didn't do what people told him to do, he would get beaten or have his food taken away from him.

Betty Anne remembered what Becky White had told her about the three kids when they first came into the foster care home. How their mother left them alone with no food or heat in the apartment. They were so abused and now Jacob was a wonderful young man. He loved living on the farm and being Amish; he even joined the church.

Betty Anne decided she would also furnish the tablecloths for the wedding. "Sara Jane, I need to go into Ruby Hope and rent the tent and table clothes. I want to make sure they won't be gone since there are several weddings coming up in June." She wanted to give the couple a special wedding gift but wasn't sure what to give them. She went into one of the Amish stores in Ruby Hope and asked the cashier if she had any gift ideas. The girl behind the counter suggested a three-piece bowl set for the woman and a nice pocket watch for the man.

The following day, Betty Anne made an appointment to see her heart doctor. After her exam, he said. "You need to slow down a little, your heart has gotten weaker than it was before your last check up; and you aren't getting any younger." She was seventy-four years old now and just couldn't slow down. Between working with the kids at the state home, and her garden, she stayed busy all the time. And now she was helping with Jacob's wedding. When was she ever going to have time to slow down?

Chapter Sixteen

Sara Jane continued with her plans for the wedding. As the wedding day became closer, she began to plan the menu. In her heart, she wished they had electricity in their home: it would make her baking so much easier. They had spoken of gas power for the stove and generated power for the refrigeration before. Levi told Sara Jane that business was good, and he thought they should go ahead and get the generated power for the farm. Since they had so many children and she loved to bake; it was past time he did something about it.

Amish America Newsletter

The Amish approach to electricity is somewhat complicated. Almost all Amish groups forgo using power from the public grid. But the Amish do rely on a variety of other sources to generate electric power.

They had been using battery powered lamps in the home for some time now. When they went out at night, they used gas lanterns. She was thrilled to know she didn't have to use the wood burning stove any longer. The new stove would be easier to use when baking the wedding cake. She said. "Levi I can hardly wait to get the new stove and refrigerator. Most of our neighbors have already converted to the gas stoves and love baking on them." The family had to use ice in their icebox before; but now it would be so much better for the family.

She was anxious to start baking on her new stove.

Levi decided to go ahead and have the Amish company in Ruby Hope to come and install the new gas-powered stove and refrigerator. He knew in his heart how much easier it would be for Sara Jane. She loved to bake and now with the wedding coming up she needed the extra help.

Sara Jane was thrilled when the men came to the farm to install the new appliances. She hugged Levi and thanked him for making the decision to go ahead with the installation.

The following month became very hectic for everyone in the family. Cindy and Daisy were helping Sara Jane make their new dresses for the wedding. She had already taught them how to sew and mend their clothes. All the Amish girls in the community knew how to cook, clean and sew at a very early age. Cindy was eleven and ready to join the quilting group. She was anxious to learn how to quilt and wanted to make one for her bed. Grace Fisher had decided she wanted light blue colors for her wedding, so Sara Jane had gone into town and bought several yards of light blue material.

Time was getting close for Jacob's wedding and Sara Jane began to feel overwhelmed a little with all the things she needed to do. Betty Anne had taken care of the tables, table clothes and the flowers. She said. "Betty Anne, I am so grateful to you and can't thank you enough for all the things you have done for us."

"You know I love all of your children, and would do anything for them. Jacob has turned out to be a fine young man and I know he's going to make Grace a good husband." They had both been baptized into the Amish tradition; and she was so proud of them.

Time was running out and the wedding day was approaching rapidly. Sara Jane had a few things left to do, but overall, she was ready for the wedding day. The boys would wear their blue shirts, black suit and black straw hats. She couldn't be prouder of them. Jacob had asked Levi, Samuel, Samuel John and Joseph Levi to stand by him during the wedding. She was worried about Samuel John standing for so long, since his legs were still weak, and he was still dependent on the cane Levi made for him. She would make sure his wheelchair was nearby.

The wedding day was here, and Cindy and Daisy looked beautiful in their new blue Amish dresses, white starched apron and white Kapp. Betty Anne had decorated the tables with lovely blue table clothes. The women folk had wrapped beautiful white ribbons around all the trees in the yard. It was a lovely sunny day with all of Sara Jane's flowers blooming around the side of the house. The two women stood looking out over the yard with tears rolling down their cheeks. They hugged each other as Betty Anne said. "This is going to be a beautiful wedding for Jacob and I am so proud to be a part of it."

Chapter Seventeen

The wedding day arrived and of course everyone including Betty Anne was nervous.

She said. "I never thought I would be so nervous at Jacob's wedding and I can't seem to stop crying." All the girls lined up on one side of the yard and the boys lined up on the other side. The Bishop stood in the middle. Jacob and Grace walked hand in hand between the boys and girls; as they stood in front of the Bishop. Sara Jane was crying and whispered in Betty Anne's ear, "If it had not been for you, this beautiful day would not have happened. They hugged each other and put their heads together as they cried.

After the wedding was over, everyone lined up at the long food table. Jacob got his wish; there on the table was fried chicken, gravy, creamed potatoes, corn on the cobb and green beans. There were other things too, such as mac and cheese. He looked at his Mother and said. "I can't believe all this food. We could feed the whole Amish community and the town of Ruby Hope." They burst out laughing as everyone looked at them. At that moment neither one of them cared.

The following weeks were hot and muggy as Jacob continued to work with Levi and Samuel in the blacksmith shop. Joseph Levi was working at the animal clinic while studying for his Veterinary Certification. He was doing good considering he only had an eighth grade education. The clinic was only two miles from the farm so he would walk home during the summer months. Jacob would drive his buggy down the road after work and see Joseph Levi walking home. They would stop and talk a few minutes each time they saw each other. Jacob was always in a hurry to get home to Grace.

Grace would have Jacob's dinner ready when he came home, and the house would be spotless. She knew how to cook sew, and clean; and was proud of their little house. Jacob couldn't wait to get home every day because he knew his supper would be waiting for him. He said to Joseph Levi. "You know, you should find a good Amish wife to take care of you."

"I just want to get my certificate for now, a wife can come later." Replied Joseph Levi.

One afternoon, Sara Jane asked Joseph Levi if he could take Samuel John to the clinic for his therapy. Joseph Levi was also due for his exam with his nephrologist. The following day, Joseph Levi hitched the horse up to the buggy and the boys started for the hospital. Joseph Levi helped Samuel John down from the buggy and walked him to his therapy clinic. As he was walking to his doctor's office, he saw Betsy. She stopped and said hello and asked about Samuel John.

Joseph Levi said. "I have an appointment with my doctor but would love to talk to you another time." She was disappointed and said goodbye to him. About an hour later, Joseph Levi was on his way to pick up Samuel John when he saw Betsy again. He stopped and said. "I'm so sorry I couldn't talk before, but I didn't want to be late for my appointment." She was happy to see him again as they sat down in the lobby to talk. Joseph Levi said. "I had a kidney transplant when I was four years old, so I have to go see my nephrologist every six months."

Betsy began to tell him about herself. She said. "I am Amish Mennonite and work here to help my family. My dad is sick and unable to work the farm any longer, so my brothers, Abe and Amos help as much as they can. They are both married and have families of their own. I also have a little brother about the same age as Samuel John."

"I can't believe you are Amish Mennonite and I want to know more about you."

"I want to know more about you too, Joseph Levi and the rest of your family."

It was getting late and Joseph Levi had completely forgotten about Samuel John. He realized he had not been to get him. He said. "Betsy, I really want to see you again and talk, but I must pick up Samuel John. Are you going to be around the hospital tomorrow?"

"Yes, I will be working tomorrow and could meet you at noon for lunch."

"I will see you for lunch tomorrow, bye, Betsy." Betsy liked him and could hardly wait to see him again. He couldn't stop thinking about Betsy and wondered what his mama and dad would think about her.

Samuel John was getting tired of waiting for his brother and went to sleep in a chair. He woke him up and told him how sorry he was for being late. As Joseph Levi guided the horse home, he continued thinking about Betsy. He knew his mama and dad might not like the idea of him seeing a Mennonite girl. She had worldly ways and his dad wouldn't like that, even though he had accepted Betty Anne all these years. He started thinking about his dad and why he excepted Betty Anne into their family.

Levi accepted her because she was so close to his wife and she helped save Joseph Levi's life when he was a child. They would have never found out about his kidney failure if it had not been for a Christian woman, named Betty Anne Miller. Joseph Levi decided he wouldn't say anything to anyone about Betsy. He would stay away from her for now and concentrate on his studies. That was his number one priority.

After several weeks, Joseph had to go see his doctor again at the hospital. As soon as he walked into the lobby, he saw Betsy. She wasn't as friendly as before, but managed to give him a half smile and say hello.

Joseph wanted to apologize to her for not coming back to meet her as he had promised but thought better of it. He said hello to her and continued down the hall. She didn't know what to think and went back to her duties. He felt bad about ignoring her like he did and thought maybe he should explain to her about his studies.

Chapter Eighteen

A couple of days later, Joseph Levi had to take Samuel John for his check-up at the hospital. He took his brother to his doctor's office and told him he would be back in a little while. He went into the lobby in hopes of seeing Betsy there. Just as he sat down, she walked by.

He said. "Betsy, wait, do you have a few minutes to talk?"

"I'm working Joseph, what do you want?"

"I would like to explain to you why I didn't come the day we were supposed to meet for lunch."

"Ok, I guess I can spare a few minutes, but I can't stay very long."

They sat down in the lobby as Joseph Levi explained his situation to her. "Betsy, you see I am studying to be a veterinarian. Right now, I just want to finish and get my certification. I'm working at the Amish veterinarian clinic with Jim Peterson. He says when I get my license, I can become his partner. So, you see, Betsy, I really like you a lot, but I can't get involved right now. I hope you understand?"

"I do understand, and I want to thank you for explaining all this to me. I was hurt when you didn't show up that day."

"I know Betsy and I am very sorry but please don't hold that against me from now on."

Betsy looked up at him with her beautiful blue eyes and said. "I don't know Joseph Levi, right now, things seem so confusing to me. Maybe one day the time will be right. We'll have to see what the future brings."

"We can still be friends, can't we? I really like you Betsy but right now I need to concentrate on my studies."

"I understand and wish you all the best. I really need to go now. I'm sure we'll see each other around the hospital." Joseph Levi felt heartbroken but knew being a veterinarian was the most important thing in his life right now.

On the ride home, he started thinking, "I sure hope Betsy isn't mad at me. I tried to tell her how things are with me. I really like her a lot, but I need to finish these courses.

I don't know how mama and dad would feel about me going around with a Mennonite girl. But she is so pretty and nice; surely, they wouldn't mind. Oh, well I've got to stop thinking about her and get my certification. That's the most important thing right now."

Amish America Magazine
Basic similarities between Amish and Mennonites
Amish and Mennonites of today emerged from a similar cultural and religious heritage.
The Amish split off from the Mennonite group *in the 17th century in reaction to what one faction saw as liberalizing trends. The descendants of these early* **Anabaptists** *have formed a wide variety of Christian churches, though with certain unifying characteristics and beliefs. Though practice varies, today Amish and Mennonites share values of* **non-resistance,** *adult baptism, and in some cases, plain clothing.*

Joseph Levi continued to study his correspondent courses. During the day he would work at the animal clinic and at night he would study. Sara Jane worried that he was going to get sick from working so hard. She said. "Levi would you please talk to Joseph Levi about all these long hour's he spends studying and working. I'm so afraid he's going to be sick." Levi said. "He's a determined young man who has a dream. Leave him alone, he knows what he's doing."

Sara Jane continued to worry about Joseph Levi, but she decided she would keep quiet about it for now. Sometimes it would be one o'clock in the morning before he would go to bed.

Finally, the day came when he finished his courses. Joseph Levi said. "Dad, can I use the carriage to drive into Ruby Hope. I need to go to the post office and mail my correspondent courses." Levi said. "I am so proud of you son, of course you can take the carriage. Be careful when you get near Ruby Hope. You know how bad the traffic is there."

Joseph Levi put his straw hat on and climbed up onto the buggy. He started down the road toward Ruby Hope Valley. He wondered how long it would take to get his certification papers. He was anxious to show Jim Peterson. If it had not been for Jim, he would have never known to send off for the courses. He thought to himself, "You know, I'm really in debt to Jim for telling me about the certification program. Maybe I could build him something, like a new sign for his building. I'll have to think on this."

Chapter Nineteen

When he arrived in Ruby Hope, he went straight to the post office. As Joseph Levi got down from the buggy and started to walk into the post office; a beautiful, young girl was coming out the door. "Hi Joseph Levi funny seeing you here." He was surprised to see her but managed to say hello, Betsy. "I'm mailing my correspondence papers today."

"That's wonderful Joseph Levi, I know you are glad to be finished with all that work."

"Now I can be a permanent partner at the animal hospital." Betsy said. "Well I must be going now, maybe I will see you at the hospital sometime."

"I hope so Betsy."

It was almost three weeks before Joseph Levi received a letter in the mail. The letter informed him that he could only get a diploma to be a veterinarian tech. He would have to go to college to be certified as a veterinarian. Since he only had an eighth-grade education, he must acquire his GED. Then he would have to apply for classes in the veterinarian program. He was disappointed as he stood there. He had wanted to become a veterinarian ever since he could remember. His spirits were low as he entered the house. Levi took his straw hat off and scratched his head. He said. "Son what is wrong? Why are you looking so sad?"

"I didn't get my certification to be a veterinarian. I must acquire a GED from school and then go to college. Dad, I can only be a veterinarian tech. What am I going to do? I can never go to college." Joseph Levi, with his face drawn and weary decided he would go to the clinic and speak to Jim Peterson. "Go ahead and go to the clinic, but hurry back, dinner is almost ready."

Sara Jane had a rule about eating on time. There was a certain time for lunch and a certain time for dinner. And she expected the family to obey by her rules.

The clinic was only a couple of miles from the farm, so Joseph Levi would walk there almost every day; especially in nice weather. When he reached the clinic, Jim was closing. Joseph Levi said. "Jim, I didn't receive my certificate today. I'm so disappointed. The letter said I must get my GED and apply for college. I can only be a veterinarian tech. "Joseph Levi you do a fine job. I'm proud of you anyway. Be here early in the morning and we'll talk about the clinic." He patted Joseph Levi on the back and said he would see him in the morning.

When he returned to the farm, Sara Jane had dinner on the table. As Joseph Levi came in through the back porch, Maggie May came running to greet him. He knelt to pet her and gave her a hug. Maggie was a sweet dog and he thought how lucky he was to find her. Samuel John came into the kitchen walking with a cane. Sara Jane was always worried he might fall because he was still a little uneasy on his legs. Maggie loved to play with Samuel John and the girls, but when Joseph Levi was around; she just wanted to be with him. They sat down to dinner and bowed their heads as Levi said the silent prayer.

The following morning, Joseph Levi woke up early. He washed and dressed before heading downstairs to breakfast. His mama was cooking pancakes and sausage and had the table set. He said. "Mama can I help you do something this morning. Jim Peterson told me he wanted to talk to me about the clinic, so I don't have much time. Levi, Daisy, and Cindy came into the kitchen and sat down at the table. "In that case do you mind checking on Samuel John. Help him get up and come to breakfast?"

"Sure mama, I'll go see about him."

Joseph Levi went into the sitting room to check on Samuel John. He was still lying in bed. "Can I help you get up this morning?" Samuel John said. "I'm not feeling so good this morning. Will you help me get out of the bed; I think I'm going to need the wheelchair today."

Joseph Levi brought him the wheelchair and helped him get up. He rolled him into the kitchen and said. "Mama, Samuel John isn't feeling very well this morning." She immediately went over to check on the boy. She felt of his head and said. "Levi, he feels really hot this morning. I think we better call the doctor."

Levi jumped up and came over to Samuel John and asked, "Son what's wrong?" Samuel John said. "Dad, my throat and head hurts, and my back is hurting too." Levi looked at his wife and said. "We better load him up in the carriage and take him to the hospital. I think there is something terribly wrong with him." Joseph Levi ran out the back door and down to the barn.

Jacob and Samuel had just come into work when Joseph Levi ran in the barn door. Samuel said.

"What's wrong Joseph Levi?" He said. "Can you help me hitch the carriage up? Dad and mama need to get Samuel John to the hospital. He is sick this morning."

Jacob and Samuel ran over to the horse and started hitching him up to the carriage as Joseph Levi helped them with the reins. They got the carriage out of the barn and parked it in front of the house. Joseph Levi said. "Thanks, I will let y'all know what happens." Samuel and Jacob were worried about Samuel John but knew they needed to stay behind and continue with the shop work. They knew Levi would want them to keep working. There would be customers coming into the shop today, too.

Joseph Levi knew he had to let Jim Peterson know he was going to be late this morning.

So, he said. "Mama, I need to go let Jim know what's going on."

"I need you to help Cindy and Daisy get off to school this morning."

"Ok mama I will do as you ask. Then I will go to the clinic."

"We will send word somehow and let all of you know about Samuel John."

Chapter Twenty

He told Jim what had happened and apologized for being late for work. "Don't worry about it, I understand. I want to talk to you this morning about becoming a partner in the clinic. I need someone like you I can depend on to run this clinic when I'm not around. And now that you are a veterinarian tech, I want to offer you that position." Joseph Levi wasn't sure what a position was. "Ok Jim, what exactly is a position? I've never heard the word before." Jim knew the Amish were not businesspeople, so, he explained the word to Joseph Levi. "You will be in charge whenever I'm not here; and will have the authority to make decisions about the clinic."

"Thank you Jim I would be pleased to be your partner but I'm not a certified vet."

"I have seen what you can do and how caring you are with the animals. I really don't care if you are certified or not. You are a natural born veterinarian and I can teach you anything you need to know about the clinic." Now all we must do is draw up a contract between you and me. That will make it legal."

After arriving at the hospital, the nurse at the information desk called Doctor Huddleston's office and spoke with his nurse. She wanted to let him know about Samuel John.

The doctor came down from his office and met Levi and Sara Jane in the emergency room. He told them that he needed to run some tests on the boy. He ordered one of the nurses to take Samuel John to get a cat scan of his neck and back. Doctor Huddleston said. "Levi, Sara Jane, I have a suspicion that Samuel John might have a spinal infection. If this is the case, he will have to be admitted to the hospital. We will need to treat him with heavy antibiotics."

Sara Jane was having a hard time understanding all of this. She told Levi she was going to go call Betty Anne. "She understands all this doctor talk and can explain it to us." Levi agreed and told her to call her to come to the hospital right away. Sara Jane went out into the lobby to find a phone. She finally found one and called Betty Anne. She said. "Betty Anne can you come to the hospital, Samuel John is sick with a spinal infection; and Levi and I need your guidance."

Betty Anne immediately grabbed her car keys and ran out the door. She arrived at the hospital within thirty minutes.

Sara Jane and Levi were still in the emergency room waiting for the results of the cat scan. She saw Betty Anne coming down the hall and ran out to meet her. They hugged as Sara Jane cried and said. "Oh Betty Anne, the doctor thinks Samuel John might have a spinal infection. They have taken him to have something called a cat scan. It could be caused by his spinal cord injury." She put her arms around Sara Jane as they sat down to wait for the results of the test. They lowered their heads and said a prayer for Samuel John.

"Lord, please be with Samuel John and watch over him and help him to be well again. Bless this family and give them the strength they need to get through this crisis. Amen."

They had waited almost two hours when the results finally came in. Doctor Huddleston came into the room where they were. He said. "It's just as I suspected, the boy does have a spinal infection. He will need to stay in the hospital until we can get this under control. I believe this is a result of his fall a couple of years ago. The infection may have been lingering in his spine all along. Perhaps it may have even had something to do with the weakness in his legs."

Know our Back. Org. / Spinal Infections / Patient Education Committee

The vertebral column (bones), the intervertebral discs, the Dural sac (the covering around the spinal cord) or the space around the spinal cord may become infected in a number of circumstances. The infection may be caused by bacteria or fungal organisms.

They couldn't believe it and put their arms around each other for support. She said. "He will be ok Sara Jane. You and Levi are good people and have a lot of faith. Why don't we say another prayer for him?" So, they huddled together as Levi spoke. *"Lord, please help Samuel John be strong and overcome this infection. Please bless him and help him to* get well, and Lord, please help Sara Jane and our family be strong and have faith."

They waited in the emergency room with Samuel John while the nurses got him a room ready. The hospital was almost filled up due to an accident on the highway. They heard someone say it was caused by a big tractor-trailer truck which had jack-knifed and created a ten- car pileup. So many people were hurt and two were dead. Betty Anne said. "That is a horrible thing to happen. Oh, those poor people. I feel so bad for them." She shut her eyes and said a silent prayer for the people that were in the wreck.

Finally, around 6:00 pm that afternoon, the nurse told Levi and Sara Jane, they had a room for Samuel John. The nurses lifted him onto a gurney and rolled him into the elevator.

Levi, Sara Jane and Betty Anne followed behind them. The nurses got him all settled in and began to take his vitals. The days that followed were critical for Samuel John. He became worse before he got better. The nurses were giving him I V's with antibiotics and trying to keep him as comfortable as they could. His back was continually hurting him. He cried for his mama and dad all the time.

Sara Jane was beside herself. She said. "Levi, I want to stay at the hospital with Samuel John. I think he gets scared at night and he needs his mama there."

"Who is going to do the cooking and getting the girls off to school?" She replied. "I thought I would call one of my cousins to come and stay with us for a few days. I'm sure Susan or Mary would love to come and help us." Levi wasn't pleased about the situation, but he agreed for her to stay with Samuel John.

He thought about the first time Samuel John was in the hospital. He cried and cried all the time because he wanted to go home.

Sara Jane gave Susan a call from the phone booth down the road. "Hi Susan, this is Sara Jane. I need a favor from you. Samuel John is sick and in the hospital, and I want to go and stay there with him for a few days. Could you come and take care of the girls and the meals for me?" Susan replied. "I would be more than happy to, Sara Jane. I am so sorry to hear about Samuel John. Our family will be praying for his recovery."

"Thank you, Susan, Levi and I really appreciate your help."

Susan arrived that evening just in time to have dinner with the family. Daisy and Cindy liked her and wouldn't stop talking to her. Finally, Levi had to tell them to stop talking her ear off. Cindy said. "Susan, are you going to stay with us while mama is gone?"

"Yes, I am Cindy and when you get home from school, I will play some games with you, if you like?" Daisy and Cindy got excited and said they couldn't wait.

Chapter Twenty-One

The following morning Levi hitched up the horse to the carriage and helped Sara Jane get inside. She was silent for most of the ride to the hospital. Levi said. "Sara Jane are you sure you want to stay at the hospital?"

"I will be fine Levi; Samuel John needs me to be with him right now. I'm only going to stay until his fever goes away and they say his infection is improving."

"We sure spend a lot of time at this hospital. Do you think God is testing us?"

"Levi how can you say that? God has blessed this family in so many ways. He's going to help Samuel John get well, so stop thinking things like that. Were Amish and you should never question your faith."

Levi walked up to Samuel John's room with Sara Jane. He was asleep when they went into the room. The nurse came in to check on him and saw Levi and Sara Jane. She asked, "Are y'all his parents?" Sara Jane said. "Yes, we are, and I am going to stay with him for a few days."

The nurse responded, "Ok ma'am, I will bring a cot in for you to sleep on while you are here."

"Thank you that would be nice of you."

They sat down in a chair and waited by Samuel John's bed until he woke up. He was drowsy and said. "Mama, dad is that you?"

"Yes son, we are both here." Samuel John was so happy to see them and reached up to put his arms around his mama. "How are you feeling today?"

"I don't feel good mama. My back is hurting." Tears ran down her face as she tried to turn away from him, so he couldn't see her cry.

"Samuel John, I have some good news for you. I'm going to stay here with you for a few days. Just until you get better. What do you think about that?" He grabbed his mama and said.

"Oh, mama I'm so glad you are staying with me. I get scared sometimes. I don't like being here alone."

"I know son, that's why I'm going to stay with you." Sara Jane had been staying at the hospital with Samuel John for three days. She was tired and worn out from sleeping on the cot but was pleased to see her son improving. A wisp of blond hair was sticking out of her head covering as she tried to tuck it back under her kappa.

The antibiotics were helping, and the infection was clearing up. Sara Jane and Levi knew their prayers were being answered. Betty Anne came to the hospital every day to see Samuel John. She would stay in his room with him while Sara Jane took a break. She would go outside and walk around the grounds and sit on a bench. She loved listening to the birds sing in the trees as the wind would blow the leaves back and forth. She would say a silent prayer for her son to get well as tears ran down her face.

On the fourth day, Doctor Huddleston came into Samuel John's room. "Samuel John you have improved so much I'm thinking about letting you go home. What do you think about that young man?" The child was so happy and said. "Oh, thank you doctor. I do want to go home with my mama." Doctor Huddleston said. "Ok then, you may go home in the morning. Now I want you to continue to take the medication I'm going to give you until it's all gone, ok?"

"Yes sir, I will." After the doctor left the room, the three of them huddled together and Sara Jane said a prayer thanking God for making Samuel John well again.

Prayer for family protection (a family prayer from www.lords-prayer-words.com)

Lord be beside us, all every dayForgiving our mistakes and making us new.
Guiding and leading us gently always.Jesus, be within us, this family is yours
Lord be above us, help us to seeNow and forever, you are our Lord.
The hope of the future, of all we could be.
Lord be beneath us, carry us when
We're too shattered or tired to really have strength.
Lord be ahead of us, smoothing our paths
Protecting and blessing the places we pass.
Lord be behind us, healing our wounds,

The following morning Betty Anne showed up to take Sara Jane and Samuel John home to the farm. As she drove out to the farm, she said. "Sara Jane, I have been so worried about Samuel John. I prayed for him every night." Sara Jane was so grateful to her and kissed her on the cheek. They all just sat back and enjoyed the ride through the country until they reached the farm. When they arrived, the family came running out to greet them. Daisy and Cindy ran up and opened the door for Samuel John. Joseph Levi, Jacob and Samuel came out of the barn to see what was happening. Levi was in the fields on his tractor and didn't know they had come home.

Jacob decided he would go out and tell Levi. He ran out into the field and took his straw hat off. He waved the hat at Levi to stop the tractor. Levi jumped down and ran across the field until he reached the house. He hugged his son and said a silent prayer thanking God for bringing his boy home. That evening Sara Jane cooked a good meal for the family. They all sat down at the table and bowed their heads: as Levi said the silent prayer.

The days that followed were happy ones for the family. Samuel John was feeling better and started walking more with his cane. He told his mama he wasn't going to use that old wheelchair anymore. "Mama I'm going to try my best to walk with this cane and I want to go back to school too."

"Ok Samuel John I think that would be a good idea. I believe you would feel better going to school than sitting around the house all the time. But you must promise me you will tell me if you start feeling weak or sick again."

"Yes, mama I will tell you."

Samuel John began getting his strength back and got up every morning and dressed himself. Sara Jane and Levi were proud of him and let him do things on his own. Daisy and Cindy were happy to have their brother play games with them again. Doctor Huddleston told Sara Jane and Levi because of the kind of injury the boy had may have caused his infection. The doctor said. "I really hope it doesn't happen again, but I can't promise it won't. He is young and strong and hopefully he will walk again one day."

When Samuel John, Daisy and Cindy came home from school every day, they would go out to the barn to see Abby. He would brush her down and feed her some oats. The girls would take carrots and feed the other horses and pet them on their heads. The weather was still warm so, the grass in the field was green and soft. Daisy and Cindy would take off their sandals and run through the green grass and sometimes just lay down on it; and look up into the sky. Samuel John decided he wanted to lie down in the grass too.

There was a trail that led to the fields and the kids would have to walk up the trail to get to the fence. Then they would have to climb over it. He walked slow but managed to make it. He was determined he was going to climb that fence. He threw his cane over and climbed right over.

Cindy and Daisy were amazed at him and couldn't wait to tell dad and mama. Samuel John said. "I made it Cindy, look at me I made it." Cindy replied. "I'm so proud of you but you could have hurt your back." Samuel John said. "The grass feels so good under my feet; I'm going to lie down in it and watch the birds fly by."

All three children laid down in the soft green grass and watched the birds fly overhead. They laughed and giggled until it started getting late. The sun was going down when they thought they better go home. Samuel John said. "You know girls we should do this every day. It was a lot of fun."

Chapter Twenty-Two

The days were getting shorter and the nights were becoming cooler. Betty Anne was watching the weather channel on the television when the man said the tornado season was about to start and everyone should be prepared. He continued to say it was going to be a bad year for storms. She began to get a little frightened. She knew her Amish friends didn't have radios or televisions so she decided she would ride out to the farm and let everyone know.

On her drive she began to reminisce like she always did. She thought about Sadie and Emily Grace and Samuel John. She had not heard from Sadie this week and as all mothers do, she began to worry that something was wrong. She thought, "I think I will give her a call when I get back home." She started thinking about all that Samuel John had been through the past year and said a prayer that he would continue to stay in good health. The memory of Joseph Levi when he was just four years old came to her mind. He was so sick with kidney failure. Then his father gave him one of his kidneys. The miracle she would never forget.

The dark clouds had started rolling in as Betty Anne was unaware of her surroundings.

She finally arrived at the farm. The children were playing on the front porch as she drove up.

They ran out to greet her. "Children you need to go inside; there's a big storm coming." Daisy, Cindy and Samuel John gathered up their jumping jacks and went into the house. Cindy ran into the kitchen and got Sara Jane. She was happy to see her and gave her a hug. "Come on in this warm cozy kitchen and have a cup of tea."

"Sara Jane, I came out to tell you and Levi there is a big storm coming; I wanted you to get prepared. You may want to get Joseph Levi to alert the neighbors."

The clouds in the sky were rolling in fast as it was getting darker and darker. She said.

"Thank you for letting me know about the weather. I need to let Levi and Samuel know. They will want to get the animals settled before the storm hits. You better go home before you get caught in the storm too." She said her goodbyes to everyone and headed for her car. It had started raining and the wind had picked up. When she arrived back in Ruby Hope, the storm had calmed down, so she felt better. That night the storm picked up again. The wind was hollowing and blowing so hard it felt like her house was shaking. She prayed for everyone to be safe.

The next morning Betty Anne found out the storm had wrecked the whole town of Ruby Hope. Some of the old buildings had been damaged beyond repair. Three people from her church had been seriously hurt. She thought, "Thank God no one was killed in this horrible storm."

She was worried about the Amish community and Sara Jane and her family. The roads were so bad with fallen limbs and debris that she couldn't drive out to check on them. She would have to wait until they cleared the roads.

An unexplained event had happened in the Amish Community. She heard the storm went right over the community and never even touched the ground. All they got was a light rain. Betty Anne knew in her heart that Sara Jane's family had already experienced enough heartache. She was convinced it was God's will. The people who lived in Ruby Hope could hardly believe what had happened. The Tornado almost destroyed the town. Two buildings crumbled to the ground.

Three people injured and in the hospital. Even the Amish community was amazed at what had happened. The local Newspapers wrote about the storm and called it an act of God.

The story about the storm stayed in the newspapers for weeks. Everyone was talking about what happened. The weather experts were scratching their heads trying to figure out how this happened. Nothing in their radar alerted them to this unusual circumstance. The Amish community was only twenty miles from Ruby Hope and it just didn't seem possible. As soon as the roads were cleared, she drove out to the Amish community. She knew everyone was talking about the storm and what happened? She wanted to make sure Sara Jane and the family was ok.

When she arrived at the farm Sara Jane invited her in to have a cup of tea.

The two women sat at the kitchen table and talked about the storm. Sara Jane said. "Betty Anne I don't know what happened. We could hear the sirens going off in Ruby Hope. The children were afraid and hid in the cellar. But nothing happened here."

"It had to be the hand of God watching over this community. But it's good that all you took precaution. You never know where these tornados will hit." Finally, the newspapers stopped reporting about the tornado. She heard someone in town say they saw a beautiful rainbow over the Amish community. She said a prayer for the people of Ruby Hope and thanked God for watching over her Amish family.

Chapter Twenty-Three

The weather was beginning to get cooler as fall descended upon Ruby Hope Valley. The town was just getting over the tornado that had hit them back in August. The buildings destroyed by the storm were being rebuilt. The injured people had recovered and were doing fine. She was so grateful to the lord for protecting the town from any worse damage than they had. Things began to get back to normal as the towns people went about their usual business.

Joseph Levi had become a partner in the local veterinarian clinic. Everyone in the Amish community began to know him and respect him. One afternoon a young woman with a cute little brown Shih Tzu appeared at the door of the clinic. Joseph Levi was busy prepping one of the cats for surgery. The couple that brought the cat in were beside themselves. The tabby was their only pet and had gotten out of the house without them knowing. "Don't worry I'll have her fixed up in no time. She's going to be ok." They seemed relieved as they sat in the waiting room. When he came out of the surgery room to speak to the owners of the tabby; he saw Betsy sitting there.

Joseph Levi handed the tabby to his owners and said. "Bring her back in a week. I will take the stitches out then. She should be just fine." The Amish couple was so grateful to Joseph Levi for saving their tabby. After they left the clinic he turned to Betsy and said. "Hi Betsy, I'm glad to see you. Is something wrong with your little dog?" He squatted down and petted the soft fur of the dog's ears. "Hi Joseph Levi, it's good to see you too. My little Bobo is not eating and has lost some weight. I'm very concerned about him." He picked Bobo up and said. "Come on Bobo: let's go see if we can find out what's ailing you."

Joseph Levi examined Bobo. He tested him for heart worms and said. "Betsy, he has heart worms. It's very dangerous for the dog but we can treat it. I believe with the treatments he will recover. That is the reason he hasn't been eating."

"Can you start him on the treatments today?"

"Yes, I'm going to give him his first treatment now and I will give you a prescription to give him at home. You will need to bring him back in a week, so I can recheck him."

"Ok I will bring him back next week. Can my other dog get the heart worms from Bobo?"

"No, but to be on the safe side, maybe you should bring her in and let me check her too."

My family loves our dog, Maggie. She has made such a difference in Samuel John, too."

"I am so glad to hear that about Samuel John. Please tell him I said hello. Joseph Levi I am so happy for you. I heard you got your certificate to be a vet."

"Well I didn't get the certificate to be a real veterinary doctor, Betsy. I would need to go to school for years to be a real vet, but I did get a certificate saying I am a veterinary tech. I can do almost anything Jim Peterson does. He is teaching me to be able to do all the things he does and has made me a partner in the clinic."

"I am so proud of you and wish you well with your new adventure."

"Thank you, Betsy. Would you mind if I came out to the hospital one day and have lunch with you?"

"I would like that."

"I have an appointment Friday at eleven with the doctor. Could I meet you at noon in the cafeteria?"

"Yes, that would be fine Joseph Levi." Betsy thanked him and left the clinic.

Joseph Levi felt an excitement in his heart. He couldn't wait to see Betsy again.

He decided he would talk with his mama about Betsy. There really wasn't that much difference in their Amish faith. After dinner that evening, he asked his Mama if they could talk. Levi was in the sitting room with Samuel John. Cindy and Daisy had gone up to bed. Sara Jane and Joseph Levi sat down at the kitchen table. "Mama I have met a girl who is Mennonite.

She works at the hospital as a candy strip girl. She reads and plays games with the kid's."

"Is her name Betsy? When Samuel John was in the hospital the first time, she read to him. She really was a sweet girl."

"Yes, mama that was her."

Sara Jane wasn't sure what to say to Joseph Levi. He was already working as a veterinarian. That alone was against their beliefs. She knew in her heart that Levi would not approve. "Joseph Levi, I will need to talk with your father about this." He was eighteen now and old enough to make his own decisions. He also knew how his father was about his Amish beliefs.

Sara Jane said. "I think you should speak to your father about this. He approves of Betty Anne coming around all the time. She has helped us in so many ways. I don't know what we would do without her. I just want you to be happy son. You have my blessing."

The following Friday morning Joseph Levi left the clinic to go see his nephrologist at the hospital. The doctor said. "You amaze me son. Your kidney functions are doing great. Your creatinine is 1.2 which is good for you. Keep taking your medications and I will see you in two months. It was eleven forty-five when he left the doctor's office. He had just enough time to go to the cafeteria. He wanted to surprise Betsy by already being there. Betsy came into the cafeteria and saw him sitting at the table. She was surprised and delighted. She gave him a big smile as she walked toward him.

He got up and helped her with her chair. Joseph Levi went through the food line and picked up two salads for them. He also got a coke for Betsy and water for himself. People were always looking at him. He said. "I don't think these people are used to seeing an Amish man, they keep looking at me." Betsy answered. "Don't let that bother you they are just curious."

"I spoke to my mama about you the other night. She remembered meeting you when Samuel John was in the hospital."

"Yes, I remember meeting your mama and dad. They seemed like very nice people." They sat and talked for a while.

Eventually, Betsy had to go back to her job. "It's time for me to go back to work. I really enjoyed seeing you today." He replied. "I enjoyed seeing you too Betsy. Would you go riding around with me on Sunday?"

"I would love to Joseph Levi. Let me give you my address." She wrote her address down for him and asked him what time she could expect him. "I'll see you Sunday at one o'clock. Thanks again for lunch."

Chapter Twenty-Four

The following week seemed to go by slow for Joseph Levi. He was anxious for Sunday to come and glad he was working; it kept his mind off Betsy. She was the first and only girl he had ever wanted to be with. He knew his dad was not going to like him running around with a Mennonite girl. He was hoping he would understand how he felt about Betsy. He decided he would go out to the barn and talk to him. He had a special bond with his dad and just knew in his heart he would understand.

Joseph Levi walked out to the barn early Saturday morning. He wanted to talk with him before anyone else came by. It was October and getting colder every day. He thought, "I need to ask dad if I can borrow the enclosed carriage tomorrow." Levi was busy putting oats in the buckets for the horses when Joseph Levi walked in. He looked up and said, "Good morning son, you are up bright and early this morning. I thought the clinic would be closed today?"

"It is, I wanted to talk to you about something before anybody else came in.

Dad, I have met a nice girl named Betsy Bieler. She lives over in Morganville, and she is Mennonite. She works at the hospital as a candy strip girl. Mama said y'all met her when Samuel John was in the hospital. Do you remember her?" Dad took his straw hat off and scratched his head. "I remember her; she seemed like a real nice young girl. Joseph Levi, you are eighteen now, I can't tell you what to do anymore. You are a grown man, with a responsible job. But you are Amish, and you have joined the church. You need to meet people from our district. She has sophisticated ways, and I'm not happy with that."

Joseph Levi was disappointed with his answer. He knew his dad was right, but his heart was aching to see Betsy again. He didn't want to go against their beliefs, so he decided to tell Betsy he couldn't see her anymore. He would tell her his family meant everything to him, and he didn't want to go against his father's faith. He hoped she would understand.

The following morning Joseph Levi drove the enclosed carriage over to Morganville. He would pick Betsy up and have a talk with her. When he arrived at their farm, he was invited to come in and meet her parents. Betsy's dad was in a wheelchair and looked frail and worn out.

Her mama was a stout little woman with a jolly face. Betsy introduced him to her mama and dad and asked him if he would like to have a cup of tea with them. Joseph Levi felt very comfortable around these people. Hannah offered him a slice of carrot cake. "Thank you, Mrs. Bieler; that looks delicious. My mama loves to bake too."

Joseph Levi was surprise to see Betsy's dad and mama wearing the traditional Amish clothes. They didn't look any different than the people of his community. They all sat around the kitchen table and spoke about his family. Joseph Levi said. "My little brother Samuel John was in a wheelchair last year. He was thrown off his horse and landed on his head and neck. He is walking now with the help of a cane and seems to be better. I also have a brother named Jacob and two younger sisters; Cindy and Daisy. Jacob is married to Grace and works with my dad as a blacksmith."

"Your family sounds really nice; I would love to meet them one day. Have you joined the Amish church?" Joseph Levi was taken aback when she asked him this. Finally, he said, "Yes, I have Mrs. Bieler."

Note: Amish America Magazine

Amish and Mennonites are diverse groups which share similarities

Joseph Levi thought Betsy's family didn't seem much different than his. His mama was always inviting people into the kitchen to have a cup of tea. He said. "Mrs. Bieler I would like to take Betsy for a ride in my carriage today?" Mrs. Bieler replied. "Yes, Joseph Levi that will be fine."

Betsy hugged her mama and dad goodbye and retrieved her woolen scarp. She wrapped it around her shoulders and walked to the front door. Joseph Levi thanked Hannah for the tea and said goodbye to them both. He held Betsy's hand and helped her climb inside the carriage.

It was a cool day, so he told Betsy to wrap the blankets in the carriage around her. The carriage was enclosed but still cold inside. He guided the horses along the trail for a while and all they could hear were the clip clopping of the horse's hoofs on the dirt roads. It was a beautiful day with lots of sunshine. Joseph Levi decided to ride down the dirt road that led to the country side. He spotted a big apple tree and said. "Look Betsy that tree is loaded with red apples. Why don't we pick some for our mamas? I have a basket in the carriage we can put them in."

"That's a great idea, Joseph Levi, I'll get the basket. I love apple pies and my mama makes the best."

They loaded up the basket with the apples and decided to continue up the road. They came to an open field. There were beautiful flowers blooming as far as you could see. Betsy said to him. "Why don't we stop here? I would love to pick some of these flowers. Look, how beautiful they are. There must be every color of the rainbow out here." Joseph Levi pulled the horses to a stop and helped Betsy out of the carriage. Betsy picked as many flowers as she could hold. Joseph Levi said. "Why don't we sit down for a while, I would like to talk to you?" So, they found a lovely spot in the field where they could sit.

Joseph Levi decided he would tell Betsy about his father and how he feels about things.

"Betsy, I want to see you more often; but my dad doesn't like the idea of me going out with a Mennonite girl. I don't want to go against his faith; and I don't want to stop seeing you. I am very confused right now."

"Joseph Levi, I want to continue see you too. I'm not a typical Mennonite girl. I only started working at the hospital to help my family. You saw my dad and the condition he is in. I'm just a simple girl with simple ideas about life. You are eighteen years old: you should be able to make up your own mind who you go out with."

They lingered in the flower fields a while longer, when she said. "I need to be getting back home. It's getting late in the day, and I need to help my mama get dad ready for bed."

Joseph Levi understood and helped her up off the ground. As he drove the carriage home, they could hear the clip-clopping of the horse's hooves on the dirt. He asked her. "When can I see you again, Betsy?"

"You can always find me at the hospital during lunch time."

Chapter Twenty-Five

The following week, Joseph Levi thought a lot about what Betsy said. He started thinking, "You know Betsy is right, I am eighteen now and I should be able to decide who I want to take riding around. Mama and dad shouldn't have the right to tell me what I should do or not do. I went ahead and tried to get my certification to be a veterinarian. I know I should follow the rules of our Amish faith, so I think I will go talk to the Bishop. Maybe he can tell me what to do."

Bishop Isaac was a kind and gentle man and Joseph Levi knew he would know what he should do. The Bishop listened to Joseph Levi's story and asked him to pray with him. He then said. "Joseph Levi, you will need to talk with your mama and dad again about Betsy. There really isn't much difference in our faiths. We all believe the same thing and according to what you have told me, Betsy sounds like a wonderful girl. Since you have already joined the church, Betsy would have to join your church. If you had not, then you would join the more progressive church that she is associated with."

Joseph Levi had not thought much about that and said. "Thank you, Bishop Isaac, I will have another talk with mama and dad." Several days after Joseph Levi spoke with the Bishop, he decided to have a talk with his parents again. It was after dinner one evening when he approached them. They were in the sitting room with Samuel John. Dad was reading his Amish bible and mama was knitting a blanket. "Mama, dad, I would like to talk to you about Betsy. You know the girl I told you about before?" They both nodded. "I went to see Bishop Isaac a few days ago. He said there really wasn't much difference in our faith and the Mennonite faith."

Levi looked up at Joseph Levi and said. "Seems to me you have already made up your mind about this girl, son? I think you did a good thing by talking with the Bishop. I like Betsy but she does have more progressive ways. Of course, you do too now that you are a veterinarian tech and working in the clinic. You are old enough to make up your own mind about these things. I would like to meet her parents and decide for myself; if that can be arranged?" He looked over at his mama and said. "Thank you, mama and dad, I just know you will like her family. Her mother is a lot like mama. She is always baking cakes and pies."

Joseph Levi and Betsy continued to see each other as often as they could. Sara Jane decided she would invite Betsy, her mama, dad and little brother over for Sunday dinner. She would prepare the food early so they could get back home before dark. It was dangerous for horse and buggies to be out on the roads after dark and it was very cold outside. When they arrived, they were happy to see the ramp in front of the porch. It made it easier for Betsy to roll her dad's wheelchair into the house. They all sat down for a nice dinner as Levi said the silent prayer.

Sara Jane had prepared a nice beef roast with gravy, mac and cheese and black-eyed peas. Hannah said to Sara Jane. "That was a delicious dinner. You must have spent hours preparing it for us."

"Thank you, Hannah, it was no problem at all; I love to cook." After dinner Levi and Sara Jane sat in the sitting room with Hannah and Thomas. They spoke of their faith and family. Hannah carried on the conversation. She said. "Since Thomas accident he has become very quiet. He hardly ever speaks anymore. Our sons come over every day to help with our farm.

Betsy loves working at the hospital; She enjoys reading stories to the children. She has a younger brother too, so she understands their fears. You have a fine young man, for a son.

Joseph Levi is so polite and nice when he comes to pick our Betsy up. Thomas and I really like him." Sara Jane and Levi enjoyed the visit with Betsy's parents and decided it would be ok for Joseph Levi to continue seeing Betsy. She was a delightful girl and his mama thought she would fit into their family just fine. They took walks in the woods and held hands. Their romance began to blossom over the past year: and he felt sure Betsy Bieler was the girl for him.

The following week, Betsy brought her little dog, Bobo into the clinic for his check-up.

She had been giving him his heart worm medicine as Joseph Levi had instructed her; so, she was hoping Bobo was going to get a good check-up. The young girl behind the desk called Betsy to come into the room where the doctor could see Bobo. Joseph Levi appeared at the door with a big smile on his face. He was so happy to see Betsy again. He said. "Hi Betsy, how is Bobo doing?" "Oh, he seems to be doing good. He's eating much better since you put him on that medication." "Good, I'm glad to hear that. Let me go ahead and check him to see how he is doing."

Joseph Levi did the examination on Bobo and took his results to the lab to be tested.

When he returned to the room where Betsy and Bobo were, he was happy to tell her that the test was negative. He said. "Mr. Bobo is going to be ok; his test indicate there are no signs of heart worms now. But you need to continue giving him the heart worm medication. I think we caught the problem just in time." Betsy was so glad to hear what he said. She kissed him on the cheek and said. "Thank you, Joseph Levi, for saving my Bobo."

Chapter Twenty-Six

The people of Ruby Hope was rebuilding their town, but it was taking longer than everyone expected. The local Ruby Hope Valley hospital had been damaged so much from the tornado that most people had to go over to the next town to the charitable hospital. It was just beginning to be fall but the chill in the air felt more like winter. It was difficult for the workers to continue to work each day because of the winds. The news around town was it was going to be at least another six months before they could finish the hospital.

The town of Ruby Hope was in such a shamble it was difficult to drive almost anywhere. Betty Anne decided to stay home and do a little house cleaning rather than get out in all the traffic and rebuilding in town. So, she decided to clean out her pantry, which was way overdue. She was throwing things away when something bit her on the leg. Her leg swelled up and was hurting so much she could barely walk. She managed to call Barbara, her neighbor to come over to help her.

Barbara had to drive her over to the next town of Morganville to the charitable hospital. She waited in the emergency room for a while. The nurses finally came and took Betty Anne where the doctor could treat her. Her leg had begun to turn blue and was very painful. She was propped up in the hospital bed looking out into the hall. She saw a young man pacing the floors. She called him to come into her room. As he came into her room, she could see all the needle marks on his arm. She knew he had been doing drugs. "The doctors and nurses won't give me any more drugs; as the tears fail down his face."

Betty Anne felt sorry for the young man and asked him to sit down beside her bed. She held his hands in her hands and said. "Son I know you are hurting now, and feel like no one will help you. But god will help you if you will let him. He is standing right beside you now. He wants you to know how much he loves you and wants to help you get through this. I want you to bow you head and pray with me." The young man continued crying and asking God to forgive him. He asked him if he would help him get off the drugs and make him a better man. Betty Anne began to cry too as she reached out and hugged him.

When he left her room, he told the nurses he was going to be ok and left the emergency area. He went through the doors into the waiting room with tears streaming down his face. He asked Barbara if that lady was her friend. Barbara said. "Yes, she is my best and closest friend."

The young man said. "That lady showed me the way to salvation, and I know now I can get off these drugs. God is always with me in my times of trouble."

"Yes, he is son and all you must do is believe in God and carry him around in your heart. Your life will turn around if you believe and pray to him every day. He gives you the strength you need to get through another day."

The doctor came in and asked Betty Anne if she knew what had bitten her? She said. I'm not sure Doctor but I think it was a spider. My leg started swelling right away and I could barely walk." The doctor said. "Your bloodwork shows an unknown virus. We are going to treat you with antibiotics for a week. You will need to stay in the hospital during that time to make sure we get this virus under control. We need to get this swelling down in your leg."

Barbara came back to the emergency room where they had Betty Anne. She said. "Betty Anne, I don't know what you said to that young man, but I believe he is going to be alright. You saved him from a life of drugs and addiction."

"I hope so because he was in a lot of pain. I simply told him about God and prayed with him. Barbara I am going to have to stay in the hospital for a week. The doctor says I have an unknown virus and will need antibiotics through my veins. Would you mind watching after Casey and Boots?" Barbara was more than happy to take care of Betty Anne's animals.

She went home after four days in the hospital. The doctor concluded that it wasn't a brown recluse but may have been a black widow spider. After taking the antibiotics the swelling in her leg went down, and she felt a lot better. Barbara said. "Betty Anne you are going to have to be more careful when you are working around your house."

"Yes, you are right Barbara and I will be more cautious next time I'm cleaning out cabinets and closets too. I surely don't want to go through this again."

The following days began to get cooler as the fall leaves started to change colors. The winds picked up and everyone in Ruby Hope thought another tornado was coming. Betty Anne prayed they wouldn't have another storm like the last one. Instead they got a lot of rain. It rained and rained for almost a month. The roads and streets were flooded, and it was difficult to go anywhere. It brought a halt to repairing the damaged buildings and hospital.

The weather had grown colder and the leaves on the trees had all fallen to the ground. It looked bare and depressing outside her window. She wanted to ride out to see Sara Jane but was afraid she might get caught in a storm; so, she decided to wait for a better time. Sadie called to see how she was feeling. "Oh, I'm doing ok Sadie. It's been raining so much here I haven't had a chance to get out of the house. How have you and Emily Grace been doing?"

"We are fine Mother. We thought we would come for a visit in November. What do you think about us having thanksgiving with you?"

"Oh, Sadie that is the best news I have had in a long time."

Chapter Twenty-Seven

The month of October started off with the rains then turned very cold. Betty Anne decided to drive out to the farm regardless of the cold weather. She bundled up as best she could. She wore a scarf around her neck along with her heavy coat and boots. The pumpkins looked so nice lining the streets of Ruby Hope as she passed. The grocery stores had displays of pumpkins of all shapes and sizes in front of their buildings.

As she got closer to the farm, she saw a big wagon full of Amish kids. The wagon was loaded with hay and the kids were all laughing and singing a song in a language she didn't understand. She figured it must have been Dutch. Since Pennsylvania Dutch was the spoken language of the Amish people. Even though, Levi and Sara Jane never spoke that way around her very much. It was so refreshing to see the children having fun like this; and she wondered if Daisy and Cindy were in the wagon?

She arrived at Sara Jane's and saw Levi and Samuel out in the barn working. Jacob was leaving in his carriage when she drove up in front of the house. He waved to her as he passed her by. She started thinking, "That Jacob has really turned out to be a wonderful young Amish man. His past childhood experiences had not interfered in his new life at all. He took to the Amish way of life as if he had been born into it. Jacob and Grace are a match made in heaven too. They truly love each other, and it shows on their faces every time I see them. I am so happy for them."

Sara Jane opened the front door to get more firewood off the front porch, and found Betty Anne standing there. She grabbed her by the arm and said. "Come on in before you freeze.

I had no idea you were out here. But I'm so happy to see you." She motioned for her to come into the kitchen and have a cup of hot tea. Betty Anne took off her coat and boots and sat down at the kitchen table.

She said. "It is so cold today, but I just couldn't wait to come out to see all of you. I have really missed the family. How is everyone doing?"

Sara Jane said. "Joseph Levi and his friend Betsy brought her parents to meet us. They came for Sunday dinner last week. Their names are Thomas and Hannah and seem to be very nice people. They are quite taken with Joseph Levi."

"I can certainly understand why. He is sweet and kind and a very handsome young man. And he has a wonderful career as a veterinarian."

"Yes, he is, and I can hardly believe my son has come all this way. His determination to become a veterinarian has stunned the whole Amish community. Everyone loves him though and trust him with their animals.

When he was a little boy and sick all the time I was afraid of losing him. If it had not been for you, I don't know what we would have done." She got up from her chair and put her arms around Betty Anne and said. "I love you and thank you for always being here for us."

"I love you too, and you know I consider you and Levi as my family. I hope God will let me always be here for this family." She put her arms around Sara Jane.

Betty Anne said. "Do you think Joseph Levi and Betsy will marry?"

"I really believe they will. He hasn't said anything to me about marriage, but they have gotten close over the past year.

I think he wants to get settled in the clinic before he makes any kind of decisions like marriage."

"That is very wise of him. He is a very smart young man." Betty Anne replied.

"Now tell me how Samuel John, Daisy and Cindy are doing?"

"Samuel John is back in school and seems to be doing fine. He still uses the cane Levi made for him, but I really believe one day soon he will be able to get rid of it. The doctor said it was possible for him to get another infection but the longer he goes without that happening; the chances are he won't."

Betty Anne was so happy to hear the good news about Samuel John. She said, "Did I tell you that Sadie and Emily Grace are coming for Thanksgiving this year. I am so excited and can't wait to see them. She will want to know all about the kids, so tell me about the girls. What has been going on with them. By the way I saw a wagon full of Amish kids on the way here and wondered if the girls were with them. They seemed to be going on a hayride."

Sara Jane said. "No it wasn't Daisy and Cindy. I keep them close to home. They are in school and when they come home, they help me with dinner. I'm also teaching them both how to quilt and knit. Cindy has made a pair of gloves for Samuel John and Daisy is working on a pair of socks for Levi." She laughed and giggled a little as she told the story. She continued. "They are so funny when they are knitting, and the socks Daisy is making are so cute. I can't help but laugh a little."

"What time do they get home from school today, I would love to see them before I have to leave?"

"I need to go pick them up in a few minutes, why don't you go with me? They would love to see you too." So, Betty Anne decided to ride in the enclosed carriage with her to go pick the kids up from school. The children were excited to see Betty Anne and ran and hugged her.

They got in the carriage as their mama guided the horses down the road toward the farm. Betty Anne was surprised at how warm it was in the enclosed carriage as she sat back and enjoyed the ride back to the farm with the girls.

Chapter Twenty-Eight

Cindy and Samuel John were going to graduate from school in the spring. Levi started teaching Samuel John the blacksmith trade. After school every day, he would go to the shop and hang out with his dad, Uncle Samuel and his brother Jacob. They would each teach him some part of the smithy trade. Levi wanted him to learn the right and safe way to handle the forge and tools. Samuel John loved the trade and decided he would like to become a smithy too.

In the back of his mind he kept thinking about the compass Betty Anne had given him a few years ago. He remembers her saying to him that it would guide him home wherever you go.

He knew the Amish usually stay on the farm and learn their father's trade, but somewhere in his heart he wanted to travel and see what was beyond the Amish community.

He knew his mama and dad would not be very happy with him if he decided to leave the community. But some of the other kids had left for a while just to see if they liked the outside world. So, he thought he might try to go to the big city for a visit. He was at the right age to start going to the singings on Saturday nights too. He was just curious about all this and kept his thoughts to himself for the time being.

Cindy had decided a long time ago she wanted to be just like her mama. She had started going to the quilting group with Sara Jane and Betty Anne and loved it. She loved the Amish way of living and already knew how to do almost as much as her mama did. Sara Jane had taught her to bake and cook and now she could quilt. Cindy told Betty Anne, "I hope to get married by the time l am seventeen and have my own house. I love cooking and cleaning and now I can quilt. Dad said he was making me a hope chest for my graduation and I can't wait to start saving things for my marriage someday."

Betty Anne was amazed at how grown these kids had become. She could remember when they first came to the farm to live. How shy they were and didn't trust anyone. Now it was as if they had belonged here their whole lives. She was so proud of Cindy and decided she would go to the Village one day and find something Cindy could put in her new hope chest. Maybe she could find her a nice tablecloth or some bed linens. She would ask Sara Jane what would be best.

Daisy was ten years old now but still a mama's girl. After Cindy and Samuel John graduated from school in the spring, she would be the only one left in school. Sara Jane said to her friend one day as they visited, "I must be getting old, all my babies are growing up. You know, Betty Anne I have a very sad feeling that Samuel John is thinking about leaving the community for a while. I am hoping and praying he will return here to stay. Some of the kids go out into the world for a while just to see how they like it. Some of them return and some do not.

What will I do if he decides not to return here? My heart will be broken forever."

Betty Anne felt sorry for Sara Jane, but she knew it would be at least a couple of years before the boy could go anyway. He was simply too young right now. Fourteen was not a good age for him to be out on his own. Especially for one that had been sick as much as he had. She said. "Now listen to me, you have at least two more years before he makes that kind of decision and you are not sure he will. I believe he has the wondering feeling in his heart. I have felt that from him. But we are not sure, so you need to calm down and let's wait and see what happens."

She hugged Sara Jane and told her to stop worrying so much about things that may never happen. She said. "Thanksgiving is coming, and you should gather all your children around you and be proud and happy to have them here. Stop worrying about what may happen in the future and think about the time you have with them now." Sara Jane knew Betty Anne was right and decided to do what she said. She would concentrate on what she was going to bake for the Thanksgiving holidays.

The day was extremely cold and cloudy, and ice was hanging from the trees. Betty Anne began to worry about Sadie and Emily Grace coming for Thanksgiving. She knew they would come by train this time.

She told Sadie she would drive to the train station and pick them up. The day before Thanksgiving, she got up early and dressed. She wanted to be at the train depot way before they arrived. She was listening to the weatherman again on the radio when she heard him say, "There is a freeze warning in effect this morning for parts of Pennsylvania." She worried the train could be delayed because of the weather and not arrive on time.

She drove out to the train station and parked her car. She waited and waited for the train to pull in, but it never did. She started panicking and didn't know what to do. She went into the train station to see if she could find out why the train didn't show up. The train attendant said the tracks had ice on them, and the train had a problem. She asked him what kind of problem. "He said, ma'am, I can't be sure, but I think there was an accident. Several cars ran off the tracks because of the ice. Her heart was racing as he spoke. "How bad is it? Did anyone get hurt?

Please tell me, my daughter and granddaughter are on that train."

The attendant was getting a message from the train as she spoke to him. There were a lot of people in the train station waiting on their families too. The train station manager said.

"Everyone please listen to me; I have an announcement to make. The train you are expecting has had an accident. Some of the cars hit an ice patch and ran off the tracks. Almost all the passengers are ok, but I am sorry to say there were a few people hurt. I do not have those names currently."

Betty Anne ran out the door and ran to her car. She decided she would follow the tracks as best she could and see for herself what had happened. She desperately wanted to find Sadie and Emily Grace. She said a silent prayer as she drove. She prayed, "Please God, let my Sadie and granddaughter be ok and please watch over those people that may have gotten hurt."

Chapter Twenty-Nine

Betty Anne drove approximately twenty miles when she saw the smoke. Her heart started racing and her chest started to ache. She finally came upon the site of the train accident. There were several compartments turned over on the tracks. People were running around everywhere.

She parked her car and jumped out and ran toward the train. A gentleman tried to stop her. She started screaming Sadie's name. She fought with the man to let her get through. She saw one person lying on the ground with several people hovering over him. She ran over to where they were, so she could see who it was. "Thank God, it's not Sadie or Emily Grace."

She got loose from the man and started running toward the cars that had not turned over. She could see people inside still sitting in their seats. Some were walking up and down the aisles. She started calling Sadie's name. Eventually she climbed aboard the train and started looking for her daughter. After almost thirty minutes she found Sadie and Emily Grace. Sadie saw her mother coming through the compartment door and ran toward her. Mother, mother she called. "We are here, we're ok." Betty Anne saw them as she collided with Sadie. They wrapped their arms around each other as she said. "Thank God y'all are alright. I have been out of my mind looking for you."

Sadie said with mouth open and stuttering, "Oh Mother, we have been so frightened and worried. I just knew we weren't going to get out of here ok." The smoke from the wreck was making Betty Anne cough repeatedly.

"What about our bags, do you think we can find them?"

"I don't know Sadie, but we will find somebody who can locate them for us." The three of them climbed down the stairs of the train and tried looking for an attendant. There was so much confusion going on and the smoke was so heavy they could barely see where they were going.

The noise from the train was giving Sadie a headache.

Betty Anne was exhausted from walking and running around the train area. Sadie was starting to worry about her mother. She said. "Mother you need to slow down and take a deep breath and calm yourself. Let's go over here to your car, you can sit inside with Emily Grace while I try to find our luggage." Betty Anne wasn't going to argue with Sadie; she was so exhausted and just wanted to rest.

Sadie finally found an attendant to help her locate the bags as she ran a jerky hand through her hair. He escorted her to the baggage car, which had not been damaged. After almost an hour, she located her luggage. In the meantime, Betty Anne was sitting in the car with Emily Grace. The child was giggling so hard she had her grandmama laughing. When Sadie got closer to the car, she could hear the two of them laughing. She smiled to herself and felt happy to hear them having so much fun. "Thank God mother has calmed down a little, I was beginning to worry about her. I'm nervous enough for both of us today."

She tapped on the window and asked her mother to open the trunk of the car. "You wouldn't believe what I had to go through to find this luggage.

I saw so many people lying on the ground. Mother I think they were hurt really bad."

"I am so thankful that you and Emily Grace did not get hurt. I almost had a stroke when I saw those railroad cars derailed. The train master must have been going too fast around those curves and hit a bad patch of ice. Smoke was pouring out everywhere and I couldn't see anything. Oh, Sadie, I don't know what I would have done if you and my grandchild had gotten hurt." They were both shaking in an anxious manner.

Betty Anne drove the three of them to her house. She made hot chocolate and got some cookies out of the cookie jar. She placed them on a platter and sat them on the table. Sadie took Emily Grace to the bedroom and undressed her. She put her pajamas on her and laid her in the play pen. The child was so tired from the train trip that she went right off to sleep. Sadie dimmed the light and left the bedroom door cracked a little. Sadie said. "Mother thank you for getting that play pen for Emily Grace. It's so much easier to come and visit now."

"It won't be long before she can sleep on the bed. She is getting bigger every time I see her."

The two women sat at the kitchen table and drank their hot chocolate. Sadie's hands were still trembling. Betty Anne noticed and laid her hands-on top of Sadie's. She said. "I am so happy that you and Emily Grace came for Thanksgiving this year. I just never imagined something like a train disaster would happen. When the newspaper comes tomorrow, we will find out how many people were hurt. I pray that they will be ok."

They sat for two more hours just talking and eating snacks. Finally, Sadie said. "Mother, why don't we head to bed? I'm tired, and you look tired too." They hugged goodnight and headed for bed. Betty Anne didn't sleep very well that night. She dreamed about the train cars being turned over and all the smoke. She started sweating profusely and crying in her sleep. She eventually woke up frightened with her pajamas all wet. For a minute or two, she wasn't sure where she was. She seemed to be in a daze. She got up and changed her pajamas and said to herself, "Oh poo, it was just a nightmare."

Chapter Thirty

Tuesday before Thanksgiving, Betty Anne and Sadie started baking pies. Sadie made a peanut butter and chocolate pie and an egg custard one too. "Oh my, those pies smell so good.

They make me think of Sara Jane's house. She is always baking pies and cakes and the house smells so good all the time. I will truly miss spending the holidays with them, but I am so happy to be able to spend them with my lovely daughter and granddaughter."

Betty Anne had invited her neighbor, Barbara to spend Thanksgiving with them. She said to Sadie, "Did I ever tell you that Barbara has a son? He is a very nice-looking young man, but she doesn't see him very much. He lives in Ohio with his wife and two children. He is an electrical engineer and I understand he makes a lot of money." Sadie said. "Wow, I never knew that about Barbara. I always thought she was all alone. I am glad she has family even if she only sees them once and a while."

They continued to cook and bake during the day. All the while gossiping and laughing about everybody and everything. Emily Grace played quietly on the floor as she watched cartoons on the television. Betty Anne had a bad habit of buying toys every time she went to town in Ruby Hope. Since Levi and Sara Jane didn't want her bringing toys to the boys all the time, she decided she would buy them for her granddaughter.

Thanksgiving morning Betty Anne got up at 5 am and put the turkey in the oven to bake.

She cooked bacon and eggs for her and Sadie and then started the dressing. She wanted to have everything ready by noon. By the time Sadie got up that morning, she had the table set and breakfast ready. The turkey was baking, and the dressing was ready to go in the oven.

Sadie was really surprised and asked her, "Why didn't you get me up when you got up, I could have helped you with the turkey?"

Her mother said, "You and Emily Grace are my guest and I am not going to have you spending all your time cooking. Now you and the baby sit down and enjoy your breakfast.

Barbara will be coming over in a little while." Sadie replied. "I just don't want you to get too tired." When Barbara came over, she was so surprised to see all the pies the two women had baked. She brought a congealed salad and mac and cheese casserole. Sadie said. "Barbara that looks delicious."

It was 1 pm in the afternoon before they sat down to eat. They all lowered their heads as Betty Anne said the blessing. *"Thank you lord for all your blessings and for bringing my sweet daughter and granddaughter home for the holidays. Bless my friend Barbara and lord please bless my Amish family today, Amen."*

Sara Jane had been baking all week and had so much food for Thanksgiving that Levi said. "Who in the world are you feeding today, Sara Jane. You have enough food here for the whole community."

"Well, I just wanted to cook as much as I could. I really was hoping Betty Anne and Sadie would come out today. I miss her so much, it's just not the same without Betty Anne here." Levi replied. "I know, but she wanted to have Thanksgiving at her home for Sadie and her daughter. You can't blame her for that, Sara Jane."

John pulled his carriage into the driveway. He walked around to the back porch and entered through the kitchen. Sara Jane looked up and said. "Oh, John I am so glad you are here, we were about to eat. John pulled Sara Jane aside and whispered in her ear, Sara Jane we won't be eating with you today, Grandmother Ruth passed away a little while ago." Sara Jane was stunned as tears began to roll down her face. She didn't want the children to see her cry, so she went out onto the back porch and sat down in the swing.

Levi walked out onto the porch and sat down beside her. He put his arms around her and said. "Sara Jane, you knew this was going to happen soon, she was eighty-seven and in bad health."

"I know Levi, but that doesn't make it any easier, especially on Thanksgiving. Oh, how I wish Betty Anne was here, I need her." You have the children and me, but if it will make you feel better, I will go down to the outside phone booth and call her."

Betty Anne, Sadie, Barbara and Emily Grace were just sitting down to eat, when the phone rang. She answered and realized it was Levi on the other end. Levi said. "I am sorry to disturb you today, but Sara Jane needs you. Grandmother Ruth passed this morning."

"Oh no, Levi, I am so sorry to hear this, please tell Sara Jane I will be out in just a little while.

Thank you for calling me Levi." As she hung the phone up, she was sniffling, and wiping her nose. Her voice was tearful as she spoke.

She sat down at the table with a downturned facial expression as she explained what the call was about. She was unable to eat very much and just sat there with her hands covering her face. She said. "I need to drive out to the farm; Sara Jane was close to Ruth and says she needs me." Sadie said. "Its ok mother, we understand. You go ahead and go. Barbara and I will clean up the kitchen."

"I just hate to leave y'all on Thanksgiving. I'm not sure when I will be back." Sadie said. "If you need to stay the night, it's ok."

Sadie asked Barbara if she would be able to drive her and Emily Grace out to Sara Jane's the following day? "I would be more than happy to, Sadie."Betty Anne said her goodbyes and got into her car and headed for the farm. She felt horrible for leaving Sadie, but she knew in her heart, that Sara Jane needed her too. On her way out to the farm, she started thinking about Danny and the letter she received from his wife. It was so cold and unfeeling. She thought about how close Sara Jane and Ruth were, as tears ran down her face.

The children gathered in the sitting room near the fireplace. Sara Jane told them about Grandmother Ruth and asked them to say a silent prayer for the family. Jacob, his wife and Joseph Levi were already there for Thanksgiving, so they decided they would stay with the children and keep them quiet. Levi was in the barn hitching the horse to the carriage as Betty Anne drove up. He met her outside and told her they were going to her dad's farm. It was only a mile up the road. Betty Anne said. "I will go with you then and try to comfort Sara Jane."

Chapter Thirty-One

Mark had already started making his mother a casket. He wanted to bury her next to Grandpa on the farm. The old house wouldn't seem like the same place without Grandmother and Granddaddy. They were the heart of this Amish family. Sara Jane couldn't have been happier to see anyone, as much as she was to see Betty Anne. She threw her arms around her and said. "I am so glad you are here; I just know I couldn't get through this without you."

The following day, the Amish community knew about Ruth. The women brought all kinds of casseroles to Marks farm. Barbara drove Sadie and Emily Grace out to Sara Jane's.

Many horse and buggies lined the road that leads up to the house. It turned out to be a beautiful November day, but still very cold and wet. Everyone was bundled up and huddled together trying to stay warm. Barbara had just made it in time for the funeral. Sadie saw her mother and Sara Jane and walked over to where they were. She hugged them both and put her arms around Sara Jane just as the Bishop started the service.

The clergyman spoke about Ruth in such a calm peaceful way. He told how she raised four sons and what a wonderful cook she was. Sara Jane couldn't help but smile a little. She started thinking, "Grandmother was always cooking and baking. She made the best blueberry pie in the whole Amish community, but her health started failing when Grandpa passed away. I think her heart was broken when she lost him."

After the funeral, the people of the community walked into Mark's house and prayed with him for a time. The women set up a long table in the sitting room and laid out all the food.

They spoke of grandmother and grandpa and how much they would both be missed. They spoke of how grandmother loved to quilt in her younger days; and all the lovely quilts she had woven.

Betty Anne reminisced about the time she stayed with her when she had pneumonia. How grandpa hovered over her because he was so worried. She could feel the love between them and wished she had someone to watch over her and love her the way he had loved grandmother.

After the funeral was over, Betty Anne rode back to Ruby Hope with Barbara, Sadie and Emily Grace. Thanksgiving was over, and she knew it was time for Sadie to go home. She was so disappointed in the way the holiday tuned out. "Sadie, it was so wonderful having you and Emily Grace here."

"Mother, we loved having Thanksgiving with you and Barbara."

"I am so thankful my girls didn't get hurt in that train wreck. I don't think I have ever been as frightened as I was that day."

"I know mother, and I was afraid too. But when I saw you come through that cabin door, I have never been so happy to see someone in my whole life."

The death of Grandmother Ruth was one of those things that no one expected. "You know mother, the lord doesn't pick or choose a certain day to call you home. She is in God's hands now and with her beloved Grandpa Abram." Sadie decided to fly home. She was afraid of the train ride after what had happened. They arrived back in New York just in time. The weather changed for the worse and Betty Anne was thankful they left when they did. The winds whipped around the windows and houses as the temperature dropped to twenty degrees.

Betty Anne was listening to the man on the radio when he said the temperature had dropped to a record low. She had come down with a horrible cold and had to stay in bed. She began to run a very high fever and Barbara had to come over and take care of her. It was too cold to go outside, so Barbara called her doctor and asked if he could send her a prescription. She said. "I heard the influenza has been going around the valley. They say it's the worst case in years."

"Have you heard if it has reached the Amish community? I haven't heard from Sara Jane in over a week and I am beginning to worry about them."

"I heard around town that many of the people of that community have been sick too. The town of Ruby Hope and the Amish community have all been affected by the influenza." Replied Barbara. Betty Anne longed to get well so she could go and check on the Click family.

The epidemic of the influenza lingered for several weeks. Betty Anne heard from Barbara that two of the older women in the quilting group had passed away from the disease. She desperately needed to know how Sara Jane and her family were. But she had no way to contact them. She said to Barbara, "I am so worried, but what can I do?"

"You just worry about getting well. You are too sick to go out to the farm. When the weather clears up, I will drive out to Sara Janes and check on them for you. For now, there is nothing either one of us can do."

She was so grateful to have a friend like Barbara and thanked her for taking care of her.

She closed her eyes and said a silent prayer for those who were sick. The hospital was overflowed with sick people from this influenza. The doctors and nurses were exhausted from working overtime taking care of all the patients.

Finally, Betty Anne's fever began to break. She was still weak and didn't have much appetite, but she was beginning to feel better. Barbara said to her, "Now that you are feeling better and it has warmed up outside, I think I will drive out to the farm and check on Sara Jane and her family." Betty Anne replied, "Oh thank you Barbara. I just want to know they are all doing alright."

"I will be back in a little while, so you stay in the bed and don't try to get up.

Remember you are still very weak." Barbara drove to the farm with caution. The roads were wet and muddy, and visibility was bad.

She arrived around eleven am and the family seemed to be ok at first glance.

Sara Jane was surprised to see Barbara and asked, "Where is Betty Anne?" Barbara replied, "She has been sick with that influenza. I have been taking care of her for the past two weeks. She wanted me to come out here to check on you and your family."

"I am so sorry to hear about Betty Anne. Most of us are ok except Daisy and Cindy. The girls have been throwing up and running a high fever. Levi had to go get the Amish doctor to come and check on them. I'm exhausted from taking care of the sick ones."

Chapter Thirty-Two

Christmas was just a couple of weeks away, but the people of Ruby Hope Valley were just getting over the influenzas. The town folks began to get out and about but the streets in town were not as crowded as they usually were this time of year. Betty Anne was finally able to get out and do some shopping. She started thinking about Sara Jane and decided she would take a drive out to the farm to check on them. The weather was clearing and warming up a little each day. She thought to herself, "Thank goodness the bad weather seems to be over. The flu season has been really awful this year."

As she drove through town, she noticed all the lovely Christmas lights in the store windows. The big Christmas tree sat in the middle of town square as usual. Everywhere she looked she could see beautiful Christmas lights shining through the windows of the big old houses. She started thinking, "Having Sadie back in my life has made life worth living again. When I lost Danny, I didn't think I could go on."

She finally arrived at the farm and noticed Levi out behind the barn. He was digging a hole and she wondered what it was for?" Sara Jane heard her drive up and ran to open the front door. They were so happy to see each other. She had not seen her since Thanksgiving. The day Grandmother Ruth died. She had a big fire rowing in the fireplace and the house seemed warm and cozy. Betty Anne had so many questions for Sara Jane as they went into the kitchen to talk.

Betty Anne spoke softly as she asked, "Sara Jane, what is Levi doing behind the barn. I saw him digging a big hole?"

"She replied, "One of the calves died this morning. Levi doesn't know what happened to it, but it looked like a snake may have bitten her in the field."

"Oh, my goodness, Sara Jane, that's horrible. I am so glad it wasn't Levi or one of the children."

They continued to discuss everything that had been going on. Sara Jane said, "Daisy and Cindy had that influenzas bad. Levi had to go out in that horrible weather to get the doctor for the girls. Thankfully Levi and Samuel John didn't get it. And I seem to be ok. How are you feeling Betty Anne; are you ok?"

"I'm going to be ok, but I have really been worried about all of you." The two women hugged each other as a tear ran down their cheeks. "Betty Anne are you going to spend Christmas day with us again this year?"

"Yes, I would be delighted to come. I will be here bright and early Christmas morning."

Sara Jane was excited to tell her that her brother John was coming with a new friend.

"Can you believe it, he finally met someone in the Amish community that he really likes? Her name is Alice Miller. I thought he would never get over Rose from Lancaster county." Betty Anne replied, "I am so happy for John. He is such a good man and he already has that nice little house out on Farmers Road. Oh, and I forgot to tell you dad is going to move into the Dauda House now. Grandmother and granddaddy are gone now so he has decided to give the whole house to Caleb and his family."

Christmas morning arrived, and Betty Anne couldn't wait to get to Sara Jane's. She would get to see all the children. She had bought a few gifts for the girls and hoped Levi would not mind. He was so set in his ways and didn't believe in gift giving. He would always say to Sara Jane, "gift giving just isn't the Amish way." She thought, "I know it isn't their way, but it is my way and I want to give these kids a small gift. After all these years Levi should understand I am set in my ways too."

As she drove out to the country, she thought about Sadie and Emily Grace. She imagined Emily Grace under a big Christmas tree opening her Santa gifts. Sadie taking lots of pictures. She said to herself, "I almost wish I was there with them. At least I have my Amish family and I can always count on them to be there for me. I guess I have spent every Christmas with them for the past fifteen years. I've seen those little boys grow up and now the girls are becoming beautiful young Amish girls."

Cindy was fourteen years old now and had decided she wanted to be just like Sara Jane.

She loved taking care of the house and was always helping with the cleaning washing, and cooking. Sara Jane had even started taking her to the quilting group. Cindy loved to quilt and had started a quilt for her bed. She learned how to crochet and had started making a scarf for Samuel John.

Samuel John was still sleeping in the sitting room. It was difficult for him to climb steps, so, Sara Jane thought it best to keep him downstairs. He wasn't having bad dreams anymore and felt he could sleep there without his mama. He still relied on the cane his dad had made him when he first came home from the hospital. He was sixteen years old now and thought about going to the singings on Sunday nights. "Mama, I would like to go to the singings at Mr. Millers barn, but I don't want to go alone. Do you think Cindy could go with me." Sara Jane was hesitant about letting Cindy go with Samuel John.

She spoke with Levi and asked him what he thought about Cindy going to the singings.

"Well, Samuel John doesn't need to go alone, so I think it would be ok for Cindy to go. She's a big girl now and can keep watch over him. Sara Jane, you are going to have to let Samuel John do things on his own. He is a grown boy now and he will always carry that cane with him. He's not secure without it. And truthfully, I don't think he will ever be able to walk normally again."

"You are probably right, Levi. I know I need to let go so I have decided to let them go."

"Good idea, you are doing the right thing for those two."

Chapter Thirty-Three

The following Sunday, Samuel John and Cindy prepared to go to the singings at Mr. Miller's big red barn. Every Sunday evening, he would have the barn set up with chairs and a small stage. One of the Amish men from the community would lead the kids in songs. They would sing more energetic and faster songs than the ones they sang in church. The kids would clap and sing as loud as they could. After a few songs they would walk around and mingle with each other. If a boy met a girl he liked, he would ask her if he could drive her home in his carriage.

While standing around with some of the other Amish boys, Samuel John spotted a beautiful young girl. She had nut brown hair and rosy cheeks. Her smile was electrifying and made his heart skip. He wanted to walk right up to her and introduce himself to her, but he was too nervous and shy. Eventually, the second session of singings was over. He decided to be as brave as he could and try to meet her. He thought to himself, "Aww she wouldn't want to meet a cripple like me."

A few days later, Samuel John found out the girl he wanted to meet was named Linda.

She was the sister to a friend of his from school, Eli Bontrager. He thought he would ride over to see Eli one afternoon. Eli could introduce him to Linda and then he would ask her to go riding around with him. He had it all figured out in his mind. He walked out to the barn one afternoon to talk to Jacob about Linda. He wanted to know if this would be the right thing to do.

Jacob had been married now for almost two years to Grace. Samuel John thought Jacob would surely know what to do. He was always conscience of his legs and walking cane. Jacob wasn't sure of Samuel John's idea. "Samuel John, you should just wait and ask her at the next singing. She probably hasn't even noticed your walking cane. I met Grace at the singings. I just walked right up to her and told her my name and asked her if I could drive her home. Then we started riding around on Sunday afternoons. The next thing you know, I was asking her to marry me. If she is the proper Amish girl, she won't mind you walking with a cane.

"You are too self-conscience about it. You need to get over that before you start asking a girl to go riding around with you." Samuel John gave Jacob's advice a lot of thought and decided he would wait for the next singing to meet Linda. A couple of weeks went by, when Samuel John decided he would go to the singings on Sunday evening. He was going to meet up with his friend Eli when he arrived there. He thought to himself, "Eli doesn't know I want to meet his sister, Linda. Maybe I should ask him to introduce Linda to me. Then, it won't be so awkward."

The following Sunday night Samuel John dressed in his best black pants, black suspenders, white shirt and black straw hat. Levi had just bought him a nice black straw hat to wear. It looked nice on him: and he was proud of that hat. Levi said. "Samuel John, you can take the enclosed carriage tonight. It's a little cool and you may want to drive someone home."

"Thanks dad, but I doubt I will be driving anybody home tonight. Besides, who would want to go out with a cripple?" Levi said. "Son, you need to get over that, you are not a cripple. You have a small limp and need a cane."

"You are not the only boy in our community to use a cane. What about that Stoltzfus boy over in Morgan county? I heard he's married, and his wife is expecting. So, son, please don't worry about the cane. You will be fine." Samuel John said to himself, "I'm going to get as much courage up as I can. When I see Linda, I'm going to walk right up to her and say hello. If she is nice to me; I will ask her if I can take her home in my carriage. I sure wish Joseph Levi was here with me, he would know what I should do."

After he arrived at the singing, he saw Eli. He walked over and talked to him for a while.

Then he spotted Linda standing on the other side of the room. She was talking to three girls. She was so pretty that he began to get cold feet again. He looked at Eli and said, "Eli I would love to meet your sister, Linda. Would you introduce her to me?"

"Sure Samuel John, I would be happy to introduce you to Linda."

The two young men walked over to where Linda was standing. Eli said. "Hey, Linda, this is my friend from school, Samuel John Click." Samuel John said. "Hello, Linda, how are you?"

Linda replied, "I'm just fine, how are you? I heard you had a terrible accident with your horse last year. I was truly sorry to hear that. That is a nice cane you have. Did someone make it for you?" Samuel John looked down at his cane and said. "Yes, my dad made it for me, and he even carved my initials on it."

Linda and Samuel John found a couple of chairs and sat down. They talked for almost an hour. At last, Samuel John asked Linda, "Could I drive you home tonight, Linda?" She replied, "Yes, I would love for you to drive me home." He was so thrilled; he could hardly contain himself. He thought to himself, "She's beautiful, she's smart, and she likes me." The courtship of Samuel John and Linda Bontrager has begun.

Chapter Thirty-Four

Betty Anne was shopping in one of the many stores when Levi and Sara Jane's buggy drives up. They parked in front of the general store. As Levi was helping Sara Jane out of the carriage, Betty Anne shouted hello. Sara Jane was surprised and delighted to see her.

She said. "Levi I'm going to visit with Betty Anne while you are getting supplies for the shop."

He replied. "Ok, Sara Jane, I will be here for about an hour."

The two women sat down on a bench in front of the local 'café. Sara Jane told her about Samuel John meeting a very lovely Amish girl, named Linda Bontrager. She said. "He has been so afraid no one would like him because of his limp and cane. He says she is a beautiful girl and understands his situation. I am so happy for him, Betty Anne. But saddened because the boys have all grown up so fast. Jacob is married, and Joseph Levi is going with Betsy. The next thing you know, we will have another wedding."

Betty Anne took her hands in hers and said. "Well, Sara Jane, they had to grow up sometime. If they are happy and love these girls, it's a good thing for them."

"I guess so, I just hate to see my boys grow up and leave home." Betty Anne said. "I thought all Amish boys and girls start dating and get married at a young age?" Sara Jane said. "They do, but you know me Betty Anne, I'm more like you than I am Amish. I'm just a weak and sentimental mother." The women laughed and hugged each other. "Just think, you still have the two girls."

Levi was finished with his shopping at the general store and ready to go. He went outside and looked around for Sara Jane. He saw her sitting on a bench across the street with Betty Anne.

She looked up and saw Levi and said. "I think Levi is ready to go. I have enjoyed this visit with you so much and wish you would come out to the farm soon." Betty Anne assured her she would come out to visit. They hugged goodbye and the two women went their separate ways.

The following day, Sara Jane decided to have a talk with Samuel John. She asked him to come sit in the kitchen with her while she baked a pie. "Sure mama, what's going on?"

"Oh, nothing really. You know Samuel John; you are only sixteen years old and way too young to get serious about this girl, Linda."

"Mama, you don't have to worry, Linda and I are only friends. We enjoy talking and meeting up at the singings."

"I know her family and they are a very nice Amish family from Lancaster County. I've heard that her father is very strict. I don't think he would understand our relationship with a non-Amish woman like Betty Anne."

His Mother decided to talk to Levi about Samuel John. One hot evening in late summer, Sara Jane and Levi sat on the front porch to cool off. "Levi, I had a talk with Samuel John today about Linda. I told him he was too young to be serious about her. He told me they were just friends. I truly hope so Levi."

"Well he is sixteen years old now, Sara Jane. It's time he was interested in girls."

"I know Levi, but I can't help but worry. I think Joseph Levi and Betsy are getting serious now. But he's almost twenty and very successful. And she is a wonderful young woman. He's doing so good with his kidney and I pray every night he will continue to do good."

Levi and Sara Jane hardly ever saw Joseph Levi anymore. He worked late at the clinic and when he came home, he would go straight to bed. So, Levi decided to take a ride down to the animal clinic and give him a visit. He hitched his horse to the buggy and climbed in. His thoughts were on his sons. Joseph Levi would probably be getting married next spring and now his youngest boy is dating. The clip clopping of the horse's hooves on the dirt road made him ponder things he had not thought about in many years.

Levi thought about Sara Jane and the day they got married. How scared and nervous he was. Then he thought about Joseph Levi as a little boy and how sick he was. If it had not been for their Christian friend, Betty Anne, the boy might have died. His thoughts rambled on and on.

He couldn't stop thinking about the transplant and how good his son has done. He said to himself, "Everyone in the Amish community likes Joseph Levi and say he is the best veterinarian they have ever had here." Levi thought about Samuel John and his accident. He thought out loud, "That boy has come a long way."

Levi pulled up to the hitching post in the parking lot of the animal clinic. He tied his horses to the post. There were other buggies tied to the post as well. As he entered the clinic, there were several people in the lobby waiting to see the Veterinarians. They would have a dog or cat in their arms. He recognized most of the people from the community. He tilted his straw hat and said hullo to them.

He sat down for a few minutes until he saw Joseph Levi come through the door carrying a small beagle. The dog had a bandage around one of its legs. Joseph Levi saw his dad and nodded at him in recognition. Levi knew he had come at a bad time and told Joseph Levi he would see him at supper. Joseph Levi was very busy but said. "Dad is everything ok?" Levi replied. "Yes, I just wanted to visit with you, but you are busy, so I'll see you tonight."

Chapter Thirty-Five

At dinner that evening, Levi said to Sara Jane. "I went down to the clinic today to visit Joseph Levi. You wouldn't believe the folks that were there with their little dogs and cats. No wonder our son is so tired when he comes home every day." Joseph Levi suddenly came in through the back porch. He washed up in the kitchen sink and sat down at the table with the family.

"Dad, I'm sorry I didn't get to visit with you today. It has been so busy lately; I haven't even seen Betsy in almost two weeks."

"It's ok son, I could see how busy you were. Seems we never see you anymore."

Joseph Levi sat at the table long after dinner and chatted with Levi and Sara Jane. They talked about his job and Betsy. Sara Jane said. "This has been one of the most enjoyable evenings we have had in a long time." "I know mama, and we will do this again soon, I promise. I think I had better go to bed now, I am tired." His mama came around the table and gave him a hug. She said. "We love you so much and miss you." Joseph Levi said. "I love you and the whole family mama."

"Now you better go to bed and get some rest. I'll see you in the morning."

Joseph Levi was up bright and early the next morning. He hardly had time to eat breakfast with the family. He sat down at the table and said. "Good morning everyone, sorry but I am going to have to go now or I'm going to miss out on a broken leg or two." Cindy and Daisy snickered under their breath as they looked up at their mama. Sara Jane gave them a stern look as they covered their mouths, while laughing. Joseph Levi was always saying things to make the girls laugh. They thought he was funny and loved his sense of humor.

When he arrived at the clinic, the lobby was full of people from the community.

Each person had a sick dog or cat in their arms. One couple even brought in a small pig. He thought to himself, "This is going to be a busy day for sure. Oh well, let's get on with it then."

After getting settled with his white coat on he began to call one by one into the examining room.

Around noon that day, Betsy came into the clinic carrying a bag with sandwiches and a thermos full of hot tea. Joseph Levi was so happy to see her and decided no matter how busy they were, he was going to take a break and have lunch with her. The clinic usually closed at noon and reopened at 1pm. Most people in the community knew this and stayed away until the clinic reopened. They walked out behind the clinic building where there was a bench under a big oak tree.

The day was lovely with a slight breeze. They sat at the bench and enjoyed the sandwiches Betsy had brought. Joseph Levi said. "I am so happy to see you Betsy, I didn't realize you were off work today, but I sure am glad. I needed a break bad. We have been so busy lately, I have hardly had time to breath." She smiled at him and touched his hand and said. "I know how busy you have been. But I missed you and thought you needed a break from all of this, if only for a little while."

He said as he took both her hands in his. "I sure have missed you too, Betsy, but it has been crazy here lately. Most nights when I go home, I go straight to bed. Mama worries about me not eating supper and working too hard. Betsy, I am so glad you came by today. I've been wanting to talk to you about something. Maybe now is not a good time, but I'm just going to come right out and say it. Betsy, will you marry me? I love you so much and want to spend the rest of my life with you."

Betsy looked surprised. She wasn't expecting a marriage proposal today. She looked at him and said. "I love you too, Joseph Levi. Yes, I will marry you, but on one condition."

"What condition could that be Betsy?"

"I don't want you to turn into a workaholic. I want to be able to spend some time with you occasionally." Joseph Levi agreed with Betsy and said to her. "I promise I will always be a good husband and father to our children. I won't let this job interfere with our home life."

I will come pick you up Sunday afternoon and we will have a picnic. Then we can talk about our wedding date?" She agreed and replied. "I will fry chicken for our picnic and bring chocolate cake." He said to her. "Oh wow, that sounds so good, Betsy. Maybe we could ride up to that apple orchard and pick some apples like we used to."

"Yes, I would love that, so I will see you around 2:00 Sunday?" Lunch time was over, so he walked her to her buggy and helped her climb up. They waved goodbye as she drove the horse and buggy down the dirt road.

Chapter Thirty-Six

Joseph Levi was anxious for Sunday to come. It was only Thursday and he was getting very inpatient. He worked hard all week seeing one animal after another. He thought to himself, "I can't believe how many animals there are in this community. Jim and I are overwhelmed with all these sick dogs and cats. Well, I guess it's a good thing we have all these customers, otherwise, this clinic would go under. I just need some time off."

The weekend finally arrived, and Joseph Levi was happy he was going to be with Betsy.

He decided to tell his mama and dad about proposing to her. After dinner that evening, he asked his mama and dad if he could have a talk with them. They sat down at the kitchen table as they always did when they wanted to be alone and discuss something. Joseph Levi said. "I wanted to let you know that I have proposed to Betsy.

We are thinking about next spring when the valley is so beautiful. Sara Jane had tears in her eyes as she got up from her chair and hugged her oldest son. She said to him. "I am so proud of you and I know you have made a good choice in Betsy. I hope you both will be as happy as I have been with your dad." Sara Jane couldn't wait to call Betty Anne and tell her about Joseph Levi and Betsy. She said. "I need to go call Betty Anne and tell her the news. We have another wedding to plan."

Joseph Levi said to his mama, "I think Betsy's mama may want to help with the wedding too, mama. Maybe you both could plan it together. I would love to have it here at the farm, though." Sara Jane replied. "Of course she can help plan the wedding. And I never thought you would want to have it anywhere else but here."

Sunday ultimately came around and Joseph Levi was excited to be with Betsy. The weather was beginning to turn a little cool and the days were getting shorter. There was a breeze in the air that hinted winter was on its way to the valley. But it was a fine day for a picnic in the orchard. The orchard was a beautiful spot and was overflowing with beautiful yellow flowers.

Joseph Levi said. "They are called weeds or wildflowers." Betsy loved this place and wished they could build a house there. "This really would be a lovely place to have a home, Betsy. Maybe I could find out who owns this field and see if we could buy an acre or two."

Betsy was delighted to hear him say this. She said. "Oh Joseph Levi, could you really buy this place for us?" He responded, "Well only if the owner is willing to sell it to us. I will check it out first chance I get." Betsy said. "Can you just imagine sitting out on a big front porch looking out over this beautiful place?"

"Yes, I can, and I would love to build you a big house with a big front porch, too."

They spread a big blanket out over the ground and opened the little basket Betsy had brought. She had made chicken salad sandwiches, potato salad and brought two crisp red apples for them to eat. Sara Jane had made a big thermos full of apple cider to take on their picnic. They decided this was their favorite place in all the world. Joseph Levi took his straw hat off and laid down on the blanket. He looked up at the blue sky and said. "Look Betsy, there must be at least fifty or more geese flying overhead. I guess they are going to a warmer climate since winter is on the way here.

The sky suddenly started to get dark and the clouds were moving across the sky as if a storm was about happen. Joseph Levi and Betsy hurried and got their blanket and basket up off the ground. They ran to the carriage as fast as they could. The rain started to come down as they climbed inside. Fortunately, Joseph Levi had taken the enclosed carriage that day. It started to pour as the horses trotted down the dirt roads.

The rain was coming down so hard, Joseph Levi could barely see where they were headed. He tried to guide the horses as best he could, but the rain was just too strong. It began to thunder very loud and Betsy was frightened. She began to shiver from the cold and Joseph Levi told her to wrap up with the blanket she had brought with her.

They finally reached Betsy's house. Thankfully the rain had stopped momentarily. Betsy was able to step out of the carriage and run into the house. Joseph Levi called out to her that he would see her in a few days. She waved to him in acknowledgement. It had been a wonderful picnic regardless of the rain.

He couldn't stop thinking about that beautiful field they loved so much. It seemed each time they went riding, they would end up at that same spot. The field had big apple trees and during the summer months they would go there and pick baskets full of apples for their mothers.

Betsy's mother loved to bake apple pies almost as much as Sara Jane and was thrilled to get them.

Joseph Levi decided he would ask his dad if he knew who owned the fields. Then he would go and talk with them about purchasing a couple of acres. He had no intentions of farming the fields, so they only needed a couple acres. He wanted to start building a house for Betsy. He wanted to build a three-bedroom house with a large front porch on the front of it. Even if he had to start with a smaller house, he could build onto it later. All these thoughts kept going through his mind as he drove the carriage home that day.

Chapter Thirty-Seven

Sara Jane was amazed at how the children were growing up. Cindy was fourteen now and a beautiful young girl. Most all the young Amish boys in the community liked her and wanted to be her friend. Her mother was hesitating about her going to the Sunday night singings with Samuel John. He was hanging out with Linda now, so there wasn't any reason for Cindy to go with him. He was doing just fine on his own. Sara Jane thought to herself, "I think it's best Cindy does not go to those singings anymore. I think she should wait till she's at least sixteen.

She has turned out to be a beautiful girl, and I don't want her getting engaged too soon.

Daisy was only ten, and Sara Jane gave a lot of attention to the child. She had long blond hair and big blue eyes that sparkled whenever she laughed. Daisy was a happy child and remembered nothing of her past. The children never spoke of their birth mother. Grace was happy with Jacob and didn't care about his past. Jacob still worked with Levi and Samuel in the shop. There was so much work and Levi was happy to have all the help he could get. He was proud of Jacob for choosing to stay and work as a Smithy.

One afternoon in late fall, Samuel John decided to talk to his dad about working in the shop with him. Levi had taught all his sons the blacksmith trade from the time they were little boys. Samuel John knew in his heart that he needed to start doing something besides sitting around feeling sorry for himself. He was sixteen now, and it was time for him to start a trade.

Levi was going out to a big ranch twice a week to take care of fifty horses. He needed all the help he could get in the shop. The business was going well, and they had ranchers coming from all over the Amish community as well as Ruby Hope Valley. Levi decided to start taking Jacob with him on these trips. He needed help with all those horses he had to tend to.

Samuel John asked his dad about working in the shop one afternoon. Levi was happy to have him and said. "Son you couldn't have picked a better time to ask me that. I'm going to start taking Jacob out to the big ranch with me twice a week so I could use an extra hand in the shop." Samuel John was excited about starting work with the rest of the men in the shop.

Samuel decided he would take Samuel John under his wing and train him. Sara Jane was happy for Samuel John and gave him a big hug. She said to him, "I am so proud of you for starting to work in the shop. I just know you are going to be a great smithy."

Samuel showed Samuel John everything there was to know about being a blacksmith.

The boy had been around the shop watching his dad since he was just a little boy but had not worked with the forge and a hammer. Samuel told Samuel John about the time he burnt his arm and about the time he caught the barn on fire. He wanted the boy to know how easy it was to make a terrible mistake. Samuel wanted him to learn the correct way to handle a hammer and the forge fire. Samuel John asked Samuel a lot of questions about being a smithy. Samuel didn't mind because he realized that was the only way the boy was going to learn.

Levi and Jacob continued to go out to the big ranch twice a week. As Levi drove the buggy out to the ranch, he decided to tell Jacob why people call him the farrier. "In the modern world most blacksmiths produce art or metal pieces for people. Such things as wrought iron furniture. But for generations our families have always made horseshoes. These horseshoes can't be replaced by machines. Each horse must have a custom shaped horseshoe to fit them. A good horseshoe makes a lot of difference in horses. We must fit the horse correctly or they could go lame.

Jacob was amazed at all this and started calling Levi the farrier. He wanted to learn all he could about the horseshoes, so he could also be called the farrier one day. He understood a healthy horse is a properly fitted horse. He wanted to show Levi he could do the job and do it right. Levi was impressed by the way Jacob caught on. He said, "I am glad I decided to bring you with me Jacob. You have been a big help to this old Amish man. Fifty horses to take care of has been a problem for me lately. But now I have help and I am grateful."

Samuel John was learning more each day. He knew Samuel was the right man to teach him all about blacksmithing. He decided he wanted to be just like Samuel when he got older. He looked up to Samuel because he had saved his horse, Abby. He knew he couldn't ride her any more but every day he would brush her and walk her up the path a way. He knew the horse was getting older and he just wanted to make sure she was taken care of. Abby was still a healthy horse but spent most of her days grazing in the field. She wasn't used to pulling the carriages or working in the fields. She was Samuel Johns horse and nobody else could ride her.

Samuel John continued to go to the Sunday night singings. He couldn't wait to see Linda.

She would always be waiting for him just inside the barn. They would sit together during the singings and Samuel John would lean over and ask if he could carry her home. Linda was always acceptive. She would smile at him and say of course you can drive me home. Their friendship was getting stronger each time they met at the singings. Samuel John was almost seventeen and knew he was still too young to get married. But he had decided when he did get married, he wanted it to be someone like Linda.

After the singings, Samuel John walked Linda to his buggy. On the way home, he talked about his new job as a metalworker. He told her about his daily duties in the shop. How he has learned to make the horseshoes. She was very interested and asked him to continue to tell her all about the horseshoes he made. He said. "I am just starting of course, but my uncle Samuel is teaching me all the right ways to handle the hammer and the fire. I want to be as good as he is one day." Linda was very impressed with Samuel John and loved to hear him talk about his job and his family.

Chapter Thirty-Eight

Levi knew the family that owned the apple orchard and planned to tell Joseph Levi. He ran into the gentleman at the farmers market the other day and couldn't wait to talk to Joseph Levi about it. It happened to belong to Mr. Seth. He just lived down the road from Levi and was the man that found Samuel John the day of his accident. If it had not been for Mr. Seth, Samuel John could have died.

When Joseph Levi came home from the clinic that evening, Levi was waiting for him on the front porch. He held his straw hat in his hands as he rocked back and forth in the rocking chair. Joseph Levi pulled up to the barn in his horse and buggy. He unhitched the horse and lead him into the barn. He proceeded to give him some oats and water as he patted him on his head.

He said to the horse. "Good boy, old Ralph, now get some rest and I will see you in the morning."

As he walked up to the house, he noticed his dad rocking on the porch. He said. "Hi dad, nice evening for a rocking chair. It's getting colder each day now. Mind if I join you, I'm really tired tonight." Levi said. "Sure son, I wanted to talk to you anyway. You will never believe who owns that apple orchard you asked about. Mr. Seth, who lives down the road." Joseph Levi replied, "Dad isn't that the same man, that saved Samuel Johns life when he had his horse accident?"

"Sure is, son, and he is willing to sell you a couple of acres of that land of his."

Joseph Levi was so excited that he wanted to go and tell Betsy right away. He said to his dad, "I guess I will have to wait until tomorrow to tell Betsy, it's already dark."

"I know son, and it's too dangerous to drive the buggy this late." Joseph Levi said. "It has been a busy day at the clinic, I think I will go to bed; good night dad, see you in the morning."

"Good night, son."

The following day was just as busy as the day before for Joseph Levi. "I can't believe how many dogs and cats have come through here today. I think I will ask Jim if I can leave a few minutes early. I really want to go see Betsy and tell her about the apple orchard." Jim was pleased for Joseph Levi and said. "Go ahead before it gets dark. I can handle the clinic." Betsy was happy to see him and invited him to come in the house. Hannah was cooking dinner and asked him if he would like to stay. She was frying chicken and it smelled so good he couldn't resist. "Thank you for the invite, I would love to have supper with you. I have some great news to share."

As he sat down at the table, he took Betsy's hand in his as she sat down beside him.

Her father came into the kitchen rolling his wheelchair. He said the silent prayer and then asked his wife to pass the food around. Joseph Levi said. "Betsy and I have fallen in love with this beautiful apple orchard. I spoke with my father last night and he said the owner was willing to sell me two acres. I want to build us a little house there. When we get married next spring, it will be our new home. It has apple trees all over the property and beautiful wildflowers shooting up out of the ground."

Betsy's face lit up as she said. "Oh Joseph Levi, I am so happy. That is the most beautiful place on earth. I can't wait to start our new life there." Her mother and dad seemed pleased as her mother said. "I would love to see this place. Could we take a ride out there one afternoon?"

"Yes of course, why don't I come pick you and Thomas up this Saturday." Betsy said. "Why don't we all have a picnic there. Then mother and dad can get a good look at the property." Her mother said. "That sounds like a wonderful idea. I will fry some chicken and Betsy can make potato salad."

Joseph Levi thanked them for dinner and said he needed to go home before it got dark.

"I will see you Saturday around 12:00." They all said their goodbyes as he guided his horse up the road toward home. The following week went by fast for Joseph Levi. It was so busy at the clinic he hardly knew what day it was. Finally, Saturday rolled around. He got up early that morning, washed, dressed and went downstairs to eat breakfast. His mother was already in the kitchen cooking sausage and eggs. It had turned cold outside overnight. He wondered if Betsy's mother and father would want to go out in this cold. He could still drive them over to look at the orchard.

After they all ate breakfast, Joseph Levi hugged his mama and thanked her for such a good breakfast. He said. "I'm taking Betsy, her mama and father over to look at the orchard today. We were going to have a picnic, but I think it's too cold."

"You have a good time today and bundle up in the carriage." He replied. "Thank you, mama, we will." As he hitched old Ralph up to the carriage, he was amazed at how cold it had gotten overnight. He thought to himself, maybe we should do this another day."

As he pulled up in front of Betsy's house, she ran out the door screaming for him. "Please hurry Joseph Levi, my father's sick, can you go get Doctor Graber for us?" He got back in the carriage and headed toward the doctor's house. Betsy's father had been fragile for several years.

The tractor stalled and when he jumped down to check on it; it started to roll. It rolled right over his legs. From that point on, Thomas was unable to walk. He had been in a wheelchair ever since. Each year that passed, Thomas grew more restless and agitated. He had been in that wheelchair for five years and his heart had gotten weaker with each passing day.

Joseph Levi pulled up into the driveway of Doctor Graber's house and jumped out of the carriage. He ran up to the door and knocked. Doctor Graber answered the door and saw the look on Joseph Levi's face. He ran and got his coat and bag and followed the boy to his carriage. On the way to Betsy's house, Joseph Levi explained where they were going. "Doctor Graber, I'm not sure what is wrong with Thomas, but Betsy just told me to come and get you, fast." Doctor Graber knew of Thomas condition and said. "Thomas has been ill for several years now and I am afraid this could be bad. Joseph Levi said a silent prayer for Thomas and his family.

He wasn't sure what to expect when they arrived at Betsy's home. When Joseph Levi and Doctor Graber entered the house, Betsy and her mother were crying and hugging each other.

Thomas had passed away while Joseph Levi went to get the doctor. He had a heart attack so fast; no one could do anything to save him. He went immediately to Betsy and took her in his arms.

He said. "I am so sorry, Betsy, I hurried as fast as I could."

"It wasn't your fault; he had a heart attack and I don't think the doctor could save him. He had been ill for a long time. Mother and I had been worried that something like this might happen. I'm grateful you are here with me."

Chapter Thirty-Nine

The days that followed were filled with sadness. Betsy and her mother had to make the funeral arrangements for her father. The Amish community had their special cemetery and then there was the public one. They decided to bury him in the Amish community cemetery beside his brother, Nathan. It was a cold bitter day when they had his funeral. Everyone was bundled up, but the winds were blowing so hard that most people had to leave the cemetery early. No matter how cold it was, Joseph Levi didn't leave Betsy's side. He helped her family with whatever he could do for them.

Sara Jane and Betty Anne also came to the funeral. Sara Jane had baked a lemon cake and prepared a big pot of vegetable soup for the family. After the funeral, Sara Jane and Betty Anne went to Betsy's home and prepared the soup. Betty Anne sat the table and told the family Sara Jane had made them a hot lunch. Betsy, her mother Hannah and brothers sat down at the table and held hands. The oldest brother, Caleb, said a prayer before they ate. Caleb prayed.

"Lord, please bless this family and give us the strength to carry on. Bless our mother and help her through the days ahead. Bless the hands that cooked this food for us today, Lord. Thank you for our father and the time we had with him, we will miss him so much, Amen.

Sara Jane and Betty Anne went into the sitting room and hugged each other. Sara Jane said. "I feel so sorry for the family and I love Betsy as if she was one of my daughters. She is a sweet girl and I am so proud of Joseph Levi for standing by her." Betty Anne replied. "I love Betsy too, and I wish there was something I could do for them. We need to pray for this family, Sara Jane." They put their arms around each other and bowed their heads as they said a silent prayer for the family.

The following weeks were difficult at times for Betsy and her mother. Betsy tried to comfort her mother and help her get through the grieving, but it was difficult. She was also grieving for her father. It seemed like her mother had given up on life. She sat in the sitting room all day while Betsy was at work. When Betsy came home each day, her mother would still be sitting there. She would cook them dinner and try to get her mother to eat something. Then she would help her get ready for bed. She began to wonder if her mother was ever going to be the same again. She wasn't sure what to do, so she decided to confide in Sara Jane.

Betsy decided to stop by Joseph Levi's house on the way home one afternoon. Sara Jane invited her into the kitchen. She sat down at the table while Sara Jane made them a cup of tea.

Betsy began to explain about her mother and how she thought she was in a deep depression.

Betsy said. "Mrs. Click, I don't know what to do. My mother has lost all hope of living. I must feed her and bathe her. At night when I get her ready for bed, she has a vacant stare. Her eyes have dark circles under them; and she's not eating."

Sara Jane was surprised at this and said to Betsy. "I've been through depression myself before, but never like this. I will give my friend Betty Anne a call and see what she recommends.

She is much wiser than I am. Betsy, if I can help you do anything, please let me know. If it would make you feel better, I will go over to your house and check on your mother while you are at work." Betsy said. "Oh, would you do that for me, Mrs. Click? That would make me feel so much better."

Sara Jane spoke to Levi about the situation with Betsy's mother. He said. "I am so sorry to hear that. I wish I knew what to do for her." Sara Jane said. "I'm going to call Betty Anne tomorrow and see what she thinks. She knows so many doctors at the hospital, maybe she could get some information. Betsy says her mother is really depressed. She must do everything for her.

I'm going to go over there tomorrow and take her lunch and check on her." Levi replied. "That is a good idea, Sara Jane."

The following day, Sara Jane got up early, dressed and started her baking. She prepared a chicken casserole and a chocolate cake for Betsy and her mother. Then she prepared a pot of vegetable soup and cornbread for her family's lunch. After she finished baking, she decided to walk down the road to the outside phone booth and call her friend. It was so cold, the wind almost blew Sara Jane down on the road. She had bundled up with her wool shawl and scarf, but it just wasn't enough. As she shivered from the cold, she managed to reach the phone booth.

Betty Anne had retired from the hospital flower shop but was still volunteering at the orphanage. It was still early, so she was home. She was delighted to hear from Sara Jane and asked about the family. Sara Jane said. "Everyone is doing fine. Betty Anne, Betsy's mother is in deep depression and Betsy is beside herself. She is having to dress her and feed her every day before and after work. And when she comes home, her mother is in the sitting room looking straight ahead as if she is in another place." Betty Anne said. "Don't worry, I will come out to the farm and we'll go over to their home and talk to her."

Sara Jane was happy to hear Betty Anne say she would come and try to help. She knew she could always depend on her. She knew in her heart that Betty Anne would always be there for her. She closed her eyes and said a prayer for Betsy and her mother. She said a prayer for her friend and thanked God for bringing this wonderful woman into her life many years ago.

Chapter Forty

The following morning, Betty Anne decided to ride out to the farm. She wanted to help this poor woman with her depression. She knew in her heart what it felt like to lose a loved one.

After she lost her son, Danny, she didn't want to live any longer. Sara Jane experienced the same thing when she found out she couldn't have any more babies; she was there for her. She thought to herself, "I don't know if I can help Betsy's mother, but I sure would like to try. The disease affects your state of mind. A person can get lost within themselves. I don't know if Sara Jane or I can help this woman; but at least we will be there for her through this difficult time."

The days were getting shorter and colder as October rolled into Ruby Hope Valley. The shop windows were decorated in the usual fall fashion. Pumpkins and bales of hay were laying all along the sidewalks of town and outside the store fronts. The children were excited about Halloween and running around trying to find that perfect costume to wear. It was an exciting time of year with all the holidays approaching. The leaves on the trees were still beautiful with their colorful colors of red, orange and brown. Betty Anne always enjoyed her drive to the farm.

The scenery was spectacular with its rolling hills of farmland as far as you could see.

Sara Jane was happy to see Betty Anne coming up the road. She stood in the door waiting for her. She invited her to come in and have lunch with the family. Daisy was still at school and Joseph Levi was at the clinic. Betty Anne remarked that the house seemed empty without all the kids. She said. "Where has the time gone, Sara Jane? It seems like just yesterday there were little kids around here."

"I know, the house seems so quiet when Daisy is at school. I love to hear her little voice when she comes in the door every day. Cindy is so helpful to me; she seems to love housekeeping. I know she is going to make a nice Amish boy a fine wife one day."

Levi and Samuel John came in though the back-porch door. Hung their coats and hats and proceeded to wash their hands. Levi greeted Betty Anne and told her how happy he was to see she was doing well. They sat down to a delicious lunch of Sara Jane's homemade chicken noodle soup, as Levi said the silent prayer. Sara Jane said. "Betty Anne and I are going to visit Betsy's mother and see if we can help her. She is so depressed, and Betsy is worried sick about her." Levi remarked, "If anyone can help that lady it's you and Betty Anne."

The women rode over to Betsy's farm in Betty Anne's automobile. As they approached the house, they began to get nervous. Both women had been through depression before and knew what it was like. They were reluctant at first to go inside the house. As they walked up onto the front porch, they noticed the house seemed very dark inside. They couldn't see any candles or lanterns burning. It was a cold cloudy day which made it very dark inside the house.

Sara Jane tapped on the door but got no answer. She began to call her name, Hannah, Hannah, it's Joseph Levi's mother, Sara Jane. Are you home?" Still no answer, so she opened the front door. She knew no one in the Amish community ever locked their doors. As they stepped inside, they found Hannah sitting in the family room staring straight ahead, as if in a daze.

Betty Anne realized this was going to be a real challenge when she saw Hannah. The poor woman was in shock. Sara Jane said to Hannah. "Hi, Hannah, it's Sara Jane Click, Joseph Levi's mother. I'm here to help you. I brought you some lunch. Come on now, let's get you up and see if you can eat a little for me." Hannah just sat there staring off into space. Betty Anne and Sara Jane took her by the arms and led her to the kitchen where they sat her down in a chair.

Sara Jane filled the tea kettle with water and heated it on the wood burning stove. She sat three cups on the table and waited for the water to heat. She then poured them each a cup of tea.

The fire in the fireplace had gone out and the house was extremely cold. Sara Jane went out to the front porch and gathered some firewood and started a fire in the fireplace. It only took a few minutes before the house began to warm up. Sara Jane then went into Hannah's bedroom and found her shawl lying on the bed. She wrapped it around Hannah's shoulders.

Betty Anne began to talk to Hannah in a soft tone of voice. She wanted to try and bring this woman out of shock. Hannah's eyes were filled with tears as she began to come around.

She asked where she was? The two women spoke to her as if she was a child. Betty Anne said. "I know how you feel, depressed and lost but we are here to help you. Betsy has been worried about you and you must get well for her sake. She needs you more than ever now." Hannah said.

"What happened and why are you here?" They knew she was still in a low state of mind and Sara Jane explained to her again why they were there and what had happened to Thomas.

Hannah began to cry uncontrollable as the two women hugged her and tried to comfort her. Betty Anne knew she had not cried before and this was throwing her into a state of shock.

She needed to cry and get it all out of her system. After the woman stopped crying, they managed to get her to drink some tea and eat a few bites of the casserole Sara Jane had brought for the families dinner. Hannah began to feel better and said. "I need to be brave and strong for my Betsy and three sons. I am sorry to cause any trouble to anyone."

Sara Jane told her she had not caused anyone any trouble, they were just concerned about her. Betty Anne and Sara Jane stayed with Hannah until late afternoon. They talked about Betsy and Joseph Levi getting married in the Spring. Sara Jane said. "Hannah, I want you to feel better because I need you to help me with the wedding plans." Hannah's face lit up with happiness. She said she would be more than happy to help with the wedding.

Betty Anne asked Hannah if she felt like she needed to lay down for a while. She said. "I think I will take a little nap until Betsy gets home from work." They took her to her bedroom to lie down and covered her up with a blanket. Then they swept and mopped the kitchen and straightened up the sitting room. Sara Jane sat the casserole on the stove to keep warm. She then wrote a little note to Betsy.

"Betsy, I have left you, your little brother and mother a casserole on the stove for dinner.

Your mother is feeling much better. She is taking a nap and wants you to wake her up when you get home. The death of your father put her in a state of shock, but she is fine now and understands what has happened. She has agreed to help me with the wedding plans too. Please let me know if you need anything. May God watch over you and your family."

Love Sara Jane

Chapter Forty-One

Thanksgiving was just a month away, so Sara Jane began to clean the house. Cindy helped wash the windows and curtains. She hung them outside on the line to dry. The winds were so strong it made it difficult to hang them. Sara Jane and Cindy washed the windows and walls down. The weather was getting colder, so she knew the warmth from the fireplace would keep that room warm and cozy.

Sara Jane wanted to invite Betsy, her mother Hannah and her little brother for the holiday. She also invited Betty Anne and her neighbor, Barbara. Samuel, Maggie and their two boys, Ethan, who was seven years old now and the little one who was two were also coming.

They would have a full house this year for Thanksgiving and Sara Jane was delighted. She loved having family around her. Mark and John would also be there. Jacob and Grace would be spending the day with her family this year.

Sara Jane said to Levi. "I'm worried that we may not have enough room for all these people who are coming for Thanksgiving."

"Well, we could set the table in the kitchen and the big table in the sitting room. That should be enough room for everyone."

"Of course, Levi that is a good idea." She sat about preparing the table for the family. She figured there would be seventeen people coming for Thanksgiving this year. She said to herself, "Well we should have a delightful day with all those people coming. I just hope we have enough food for everyone." She decided to put the kettle on the stove and have a cup of hot tea.

It was bitterly cold outside, and she needed something to warm her up. Thanksgiving was a special holiday, and everyone could hardly wait to feast on the turkey and dressing. She began to think to herself, "I think I will bake several pies and a chocolate cake. Joseph Levi loves his mama's chocolate cake."

The Best of Amish Cooking by Phyllis Pellman Good

Traditional and Contemporary Recipes Adapted from the Kitchens and Pantries of Old Amish Cooks
The German settlers brought their love of pastries to Pennsylvania. What they learned from their English neighbors in the New World was how to fashion that fondness into pies.
Pies have been on Amish menus ever since.
Sara Jane's famous Apple Pie
6 cups apples, peeled and sliced
½ - ¾ cup sugar (depending upon the flavor of the apples) tbsp. flour, ¼ tsp. cinnamon
2 tbsp. lemon juice
1 9" unbaked pie shell and top crust
Chocolate Cake
The cake the Amish ate most at home was chocolate. It was usually baked in a long pan, and dusted with 10X sugar rather than iced.
1 cup brown sugar
1 cup of granulated sugar
1 cup lard (or vegetable shortening)
2 eggs, unbeaten, 1 cup buttermilk
2 ¾ cups flour cup cocoa powder, ½ cup
Water, 1 tsp. baking soda

Sara Jane would also bake a big twenty-pound turkey stuffed with a homemade dressing.

Bread Filling Recipe

Bread crusts or stale bread is not a problem to the resourceful Amish Cook.
4 eggs
2 cups milk
2 quarts soft bread cubes
4 tbsp. melted butter
1 tsp. onion, minced
1 tsp. salt, 1 tbsp. parsley chopped (optional)
1 tsp. sage or poultry seasoning (optional)

Thanksgiving that year turned out to be one of the best the family had ever had. The boys all went out in the yard and played kick ball, while the women stayed inside and cleaned the dishes for Sara Jane. They cleared all the dishes from the table and told Sara Jane to sit down and have a cup of tea. Betty Anne said to her. "Now Sara Jane, you have been baking and preparing all this food for everyone; so now it's your turn to rest."

She was amazed at how all the women, which included Betty Anne and Barbara got along in the kitchen. Sara Jane would never forget this special day. After everything had been put away and the kitchen was all cleaned up, Betty Anne sat down at the table with Sara Jane. She put a tea bag in a cup and poured hot water from the kettle simmering on the stove. The two women drank their hot tea and just sat in this warm cozy kitchen as if they had nothing else to do. The other women went into the sitting room to talk about everyday things, such as canning and quilting.

The house was warm from the wood burning in the big fireplace. The wonderful aromas from the pies and cakes still lingered in the air. Betty Anne said to Sara Jane. "Sadie and Emily Grace have invited me and Barbara to come to New York for Christmas this year. I have decided to go." Sara Jane was happy for her and said. "Oh, Betty Anne, that is wonderful, I am so glad you are going. We will miss you being here with us, but I am so happy for you. I know Sadie and Emily Grace are excited you are coming."

"Emily Grace wants to take us ice skating. Can you imagine me ice skating?

She is going to want us to see all the New York sites. I may never have the chance to go again, so I thought I would go this year." Sara Jane reached over and gave her a hug and said. "I love you and you know we will miss you not being here with us this year. But I want you to go on this trip and have fun with Sadie and Emily Grace. We are all family now."

Chapter Forty-Two

The weather continued to be bitterly cold. The man on the radio said it was only twenty- eight degrees and people should stay inside. "People do not go outside unless it is an emergency.

And please bring your pets inside. The temperature is going to drop below freezing tonight, and we may have more snow tomorrow." Betty Anne was listening to the man and began to get worried about taking the trip to New York. She remembered what happened to Sadie and Emily Grace the last time they took the train to Ruby Hope Valley. She said to herself, "Barbara and I must take the train to Pennsylvanian station and then get a taxi to take us to Sadie's house.

I wonder if Sadie is going to meet us at the train station. I think I will call her and ask her." Betty Anne called Sadie and said. "I was just wondering if Barbara and I should get a taxi to take us to your home?" Sadie replied. "Emily and I will be there to pick you up. So, don't worry about that mother." Christmas was only two weeks away and Betty Anne decided she was going on this trip no matter what the weather turned out to be. She thought to herself, "Surely, this weather is going to warm up. The snow may stop coming down by the time we get ready to go."

The two women had planned on leaving a week before Christmas. The snow continued to come down as it got closer and closer to the holiday. She looked out her bedroom window and thought how beautiful the snow was; as it came down.

Everything was so white and serene. The Christmas lights shining through the neighbor's windows gave her a fuzzy warm feeling. The store owners in town had decorated their front windows so beautifully, and the big Christmas tree that sat in the middle of town was gorgeous this year.

Betty Anne and Barbara were grateful they went shopping for Christmas gifts before the snow began. They both bought small gifts for the girls. They figured they couldn't carry large packages on the train; it would be too difficult to handle. They also packed their bags as lightly as they could. Betty Anne said to Barbara one afternoon while sitting in the living room watching the snow come down outside. "I believe the snow is beginning to slow up a little.

Hopefully by day after tomorrow, we will be able to go on our trip."

"I think we will, Betty Anne. Other people travel in this kind of weather. So, we should be ok."

There was so much uncertainty about the weather Betty Anne didn't know what to do.

Finally, the snow began to stop coming down; still everything outside was covered in the white fluffy stuff. She decided to call Sadie and ask her opinion about the snow. Sadie was so happy to hear her mother on the phone. "Hi, mother, is everything ok in Ruby Hope Valley this fine morning?" Her mother couldn't help but laugh. "Yes, dear, everything is ok except the snow is covering everything in sight and I'm not sure what to do. We are supposed to leave tomorrow morning to come there.

Is it still snowing in New York?"

"Yes, but that doesn't stop the people that live here.

Everyone goes about their business. They go shopping and ice skating. We just bundle up real warm."

"That's a good thing I suppose, but Barbara and I are a bit older than you, Sadie. Our bones can't take being out in this kind of weather. We usually stay inside and keep warm by the fireplace."

"Oh, come on, mother. We are looking forward to you and Barbara coming, and Emily Grace has all kinds of things planned. I promise we won't go outside unless it's something real important.

We have a big Christmas tree all lit up and a warm fireplace roaring just for you. Emily Grace will be so disappointed if you don't come." Betty Anne's heart almost broke when Sadie said Emily Grace would be disappointed. She said to Barbara. "Well, I guess we better bundle up real good Barbara, because we are going to New York City." Barbara was excited and gave her friend a big hug. Barbara said to her. "I will see you early in the morning, then. Don't forget to wear your long underwear. The taxi to take us to the train station will be here at seven am. I will see you at six-thirty." The two women hugged and said goodnight to each other.

Betty Anne had taken her little dog and cat to Joseph Levi's Veterinarian clinic to stay while she was gone. She missed them already and wondered if they would be ok. She knew he would take good care of her animals. It was clean and warm and had an attendant working over the holidays to take care of all the animals. She was satisfied her pets would be in good hands.

She decided to check her suitcases again for the fourth time. She wanted to make sure she didn't forget anything.

She began to get excited about taking the trip but had a little anxiety about the train. She just couldn't stop thinking about what happened to Sadie and Emily Grace when they came for Thanksgiving a couple of years ago. She bowed her head and said.

"Lord, please keep my friend Barbara and myself safe on this trip to New York.

Help me to be brave and strong and know in my heart you will always be with us."

After she said the prayer, she began to feel a relief come over her. The anxiety she felt before had ceased. She put on her pajamas and sat down in her favorite chair by the fireplace.

Picked up the book she had been reading and read it until she fell asleep in the chair. When she awakened, it was five am. She knew she needed to be ready to go by six-thirty, so she decided to go ahead and get dressed. She made a fresh pot of coffee while she was dressing. She knew Barbara would be coming over at six-thirty and she wanted to be sure she was ready to go.

It was six-thirty and Barbara was right on time. Betty Anne let her in the front door and said. "I am so excited; I can't wait to get there. How are you this morning, Barbara?" Her friend was excited too and said to Betty Anne. "I am as ready as I will ever be, and so grateful to you for asking me to go on this trip with you. I just know we are going to have a wonderful time in New York."

The taxi pulled up in front of Betty Anne's house right at seven am. The two women carried their luggage to the car. The driver got out of the taxi and opened the trunk. He stored all their luggage securely. He opened the doors of the car and helped each woman climb inside.

He said as he started up the automobile. "We will arrive at the train station in just under an hour."

The weather was dreadful as it started to snow again. Betty Anne and Barbara were very nervous and sat quietly as the car got on the freeway and zoomed toward the train station. Barbara reached over and put her hands-on top of Betty Anne's. She wanted to reassure her everything was going to be ok.

Chapter Forty-Three

When they arrived at the Lancaster train station, people were climbing aboard. The taxi cab driver helped them out of the car and went around to the back of the cab and retrieved their luggage. They paid him his fee and wished him a very Merry Christmas. The two women stood there just looking at the train. There were so many people getting aboard and it seemed so congested. Barbara finally spoke up and said. "Betty Anne, I guess we had better get aboard this big bus before it leaves without us." The train attendant helped them with their luggage and escorted them to their train car.

After a few minutes, the train began to roll down the tracks. It went faster and faster.

Betty Anne said to Barbara. "You know, I will feel so much better when we arrive in New York.

I think I am getting too old to be making these kinds of trips."

"Betty Anne why don't you lay your head back on the seat and take a little nap. Before you know it, we will be there." It wasn't long when the train pulled into the New York Penn train station.

Both women were delighted and started laughing because they had been so foolish about coming on this trip. Sadie and Emily were waiting for them inside the station. They were bundled up like Eskimos with scarfs around their necks and knit hats on their heads. They also had on warm jackets and boots. Betty Anne was happy to see them dressed so warm.

Wikipedia.com

Lancaster is an Amtrak railroad station and a former Pennsylvania Railroad station in Lancaster, Lancaster County in the U.S. state of Pennsylvania. Located on the Keystone Corridor, the station is served by the Keystone Service between New York city and Harrisburg, and by the Pennsylvania between New York and Pittsburgh. Lancaster is the second busiest Amtrak station in Pennsylvania, and the twenty-first busiest in the United States.

Sadie and Emily saw the two women through the window of the train and started waving to them. Emily was so excited and could hardly wait for her grandmama to get off the train.

Betty Anne and Barbara waved back at them as they made their way down the aisle toward the exit. The porter came by and asked if he could help them with their luggage. Betty Anne said. "Yes, would you please help us retrieve them." The porter took their luggage tickets and said he would bring them to the outside exit. He asked them to wait just outside the exit of the train.

Sadie and Emily ran over to where they were and grabbed and hugged both women.

Emily said. "Grandmama, I am so happy you came. We are going to have a lot of fun and I just know this is going to be the best Christmas ever." The porter brought their luggage out to them.

Betty Anne gave him a five-dollar bill and thanked him for helping them. The man thanked her and tipped his hat to her. He told them to have a very Merry Christmas and went on his way.

Sadie and Emily picked up their luggage and asked Betty Anne and Barbara to follow them to their car.

As they drove down the highway, Sadie asked if anyone was hungry. Emily said in a very loud voice, "I am. Let's take them to our favorite place mama." Betty Anne and Barbara said they were a little hungry too. "Ok, then Miss Emily, we will take them to Ruby's Café on Mulberry Street."

"The food is great their grandmama and you will love the expresso coffee and drinks. Why it's the best in New York." Barbara said. "With a name like that it's got to be good." Betty Anne said, "I can hardly wait to eat at Ruby's Café."

"You're going to love it, grandmama."

They all had a delicious dinner the first evening in New York. Emily said. "Barbara, you and grandmama are going to have a great time while you are here. I want to show you all the sites." She was such a chatter box that Sadie had to tell her to calm down a little. Sadie said. "Let these ladies catch their breath Emily. They just had a three-hour trip on the train; I know they must be exhausted. We will decide what to do tomorrow. But first things first. We will take them home and let them relax a little before going to bed. And you Miss Emily need to go to bed soon too. It's way past your bedtime."

Sadie lived on the fifth floor of a beautiful apartment building. Betty Anne thought to herself, "Thank goodness they have elevators. No way I could climb five flights of steps." Sadie said. "I hope you like our home. It has been so good living here. Our neighbors are very nice people." As she opened the door to the apartment Betty Anne and Barbara were amazed. The living room was very big and bright; it had windows all around the room overlooking the city. They had a large Christmas tree standing right in the middle of the room. A big fire was raging in the fireplace; it was so cozy and warm they felt right at home.

Sadie showed them to their bedrooms and said. "I know you are worn out and need to rest." She hugged her mother and said to her. "I am so happy you came, mother. Now you get some rest and I will see you in the morning. If you ladies need anything, just let me know." The following morning Betty Anne and Barbara were up early. Sadie said. "Good morning mother, this is Annie, our cook. She has prepared a delicious breakfast for us. Come sit down and have a cup of coffee."

After breakfast, Emily said she wanted to take them to see the Empire State Building and then to Rockefeller Center. Sadie said. "How do you ladies feel this morning? Do you think you are up to this? Emily is so excited you are here and can't wait to show you everything." Betty Anne replied. "Well if Barbara is up to the excursion, then so am I." Sadie told them there would be a lot of walking, but she would make sure they rested along the way. "I hope y'all brought a lot of warm clothes to wear?" Barbara said. "We brought what we could. I think we will be warm enough."

"Ok then we will get started right after breakfast."

Betty Anne asked Sadie where her husband and mother in law were? Sadie replied. "Oh, I thought I told you. My husband took his mother to visit her family for Christmas. He usually is here but he wanted us to be able to spend as much time together as we could. So, he thought this would be a good time to go on this trip. We had our Christmas together before they left." Betty Anne was satisfied with her answer and decided she wouldn't worry about it any longer.

Chapter Forty-Four

After they ate a delicious breakfast of scrambled eggs biscuits and gravy, fruit and oatmeal, Sadie said. "Ok, ladies, be sure you dress warmly today because we are going to be outside most of the time." Betty Anne replied. "We both brought warm clothes and I even brought my new boots to wear."

"That's great mother, you really need boots to travel around this town." Emily said she wanted to take them to see the Empire State Building first. "How does that sound to you and Barbara, mother?" Barbara replied. "Oh, I can't wait to see the Empire State Building. I have been wanting to see it for years."

Betty Anne said. "I'm ready to go when you are."

The snow continued to fall in Ruby Hope Valley. Most people stayed inside with their families. It was too slippery and wet to be outside. Sara Jane said to Levi. "I really am going to miss Betty Anne spending Christmas with us this year. She has been here almost every year since Joseph Levi was born. Levi, do you realize it's been eighteen years. I do hope she is having a good time with Sadie and Emily." They were expecting Samuel, Mattie Sue and Ethan Nathaniel to come for Christmas dinner. She also had invited Jacob and Grace.

Joseph Levi wanted to spend Christmas with Betsy but decided he would spend it with his family. He started thinking about Betsy's family, "She lost her father last year just before Christmas. I remember her family spent the holiday with my family; so, this would be their first Christmas at home without her father. I think it would be best if I go later to see her. I want her to be able to be with her family today."

The couple had decided to get married in the spring. Joseph Levi had already spoke with Mr. Seth about purchasing the orchard property. He would have to wait until the weather got better before getting started on the house. His heart was set on building the house before the wedding, but the weather was so bad he would have to wait. Since he became a partner with Jim Peterson, he had been saving all the money he earned at the clinic. He had saved enough money to build a nice house for Betsy. He knew the house would have to be small to begin with but decided he would build onto it later.

The orchard property was a beautiful place to have a home built and he couldn't stop thinking about it. Betsy was excited about the wedding and the house. She was so happy when he told her he had been able to purchase two acres from Mr. Seth. The orchard was the couple's favorite place and she knew they would be happy there. Sara Jane had cooked a feast as usual for Christmas day. She had been baking pies all week and had a nice fat turkey ready to roast. She loved the new stove Levi had bought her last year. It had made her baking so much easier.

She had set up a long table in the big sitting room and Cindy and Daisy brought chairs in from the kitchen. The two girls also sat the table for her. She was proud of them and thanked them for being her helpers. Cindy was fifteen now with blond hair and blue eyes. The young men in the Amish Community were always whispering about her whenever she was around. But Cindy wasn't interested in boys and didn't pay them any attention. She loved keeping house and helping her mama with the chores.

After Christmas was over, Sara Jane took the girls into Ruby Hope Valley for a shopping day. She needed to go to the market to pick up staples such as flour and sugar. The girls decided to walk over to the ice cream parlor. Sara Jane gave them enough money to buy some candy or an ice cream cone. It was still extremely cold outside, but the snow had stopped coming down.

The girls were bundled up with their Amish wool shawls boots and stockings. They sat down at one of the small tables and ordered a chocolate ice cream cone. The young man working behind the counter was also Amish. He liked Cindy and told them the ice cream was free.

He couldn't stop staring at her. He thought she was the most beautiful girl he had ever seen. The girls thanked him for the ice cream and said they had to go meet their mama. He said to Cindy. "My name is Eli Lapp and I was wondering if you ever go to the singings at Church?

Cindy hesitated with her remarks. "I went with my brother once. But my mama doesn't think I'm old enough to start going. We have to go now." Eli was disappointed that the girls had to leave.

He really wanted to get to know Cindy. He knew Samuel John and decided he would ask him to bring his sister next time he came to the singings.

Cindy and Daisy crossed the street that led to the market. Sara Jane had finished her shopping and was ready to go. "I think I will stop by the fabric shop and pick up some new material. You girls need a new dress." Cindy and Daisy were excited about the new dresses.

Cindy asked if she could have a new purple dress. Sara Jane said. "That is my favorite color too, Cindy. Yes, I will buy some purple material just for you. What about you Daisy? What color do you like?" Daisy looked down at the ground with a wide grin on her face. Her eyes sparkled and gleamed with excitement. "Pink, I want pink, mama."

"Well then, Miss Daisy, pink it is.

I will make a purple dress with a new white apron for Cindy and pink dress for you." The girls ran and hugged their mama and thanked her for the new material. As they were heading home in the buggy, Daisy said. "Mama, a boy at the ice cream shop talked to Cindy. He wanted to know if she went to the singings. What does that mean mama?" Sara Jane asked Cindy what the young man said to her? Cindy said. "His name is Eli Lapp, mama. He wanted to know if I ever go to the singings at church." "Oh, so he is an Amish boy? What did you say to him?"

"I told him I had gone once with Samuel John. Nothing else mama."

"You know I don't like you talking to strange boys, Cindy. And you are too young to go to the singings. Maybe next year you can go, but right now, you are too young."

"Ok, mama, I don't want to go anyway. I don't really like boys, but Eli was nice wasn't he, Daisy?"

"Yes, but what does singings mean?"

Chapter Forty-Five

After breakfast, Betty Anne and Barbara dressed for the day. Sadie told them to dress warmly so they put on heavy sweaters, puffed jackets, boots and scarps around their necks.

Barbara said. "We should be fine outside today with all this winter apparel on."

"I'm just worried about all the walking. I'm not as young as I used to be." Replied Betty Anne. Emily was excited and ready to go. Sadie said. "Let's go everybody, the ferry leaves in half an hour. We must take the ferry over to the island to see the statue of Liberty."

Sadie got them a cab to take them to the ferry where they could go and see the Statue of Liberty. Betty Anne and Barbara's faces were beaming with excitement. Betty Anne's heart rate was racing as she boarded the ferry. The two women couldn't believe they were about to see Ellis Island. Betty Anne said. "I can't believe I have lived this close to New York and never been here to see this before. This is amazing and something I will never forget." Emily hugged her grandmama and said. "I am so happy you came for Christmas this year. I have missed you so much."

Emily Grace was twelve years old now and tuned out to be a beautiful young girl.

She was sweet and well behaved. Betty Anne was so proud of her and thanked God every day for reuniting her with her daughter, Sadie. After they returned to the mainland and got off the ferry, they decided to walk. Sadie said. "I have an idea that I just know you will love. Let's walk across the Brooklyn Bridge. Then we will stop at one of the local restaurants and have lunch."

Emily chimed in and said. "That sounds fabulous, mama. Let's do it."

Sadie asked her mother if she thought she was up to the walk. "It sounds like fun, so I will try and make it."

"You have to walk across the Brooklyn Bridge at least once in your life if you come to New York." Replied Sadie. After they had their walk, they stopped at a delightful small restaurant called Cheddar's, for lunch. The food was delicious, and Betty Anne and Barbara were having a wonderful time. Everyone was trying to talk all at once. Emily was so excited she began to get the giggles. Sadie cautioned her to stop talking so much. After lunch was over, the women decided to walk a little way down the street and catch a taxi.

Betty Anne was getting tired and Sadie could tell she needed to rest. Sadie knew about her mother's heart condition and she didn't want her to get worn out the first day, so she said.

"Emily, I believe grandmama is getting tired and since we have already had a long day, why don't we go home and start over tomorrow?" Emily tried to understand but she wasn't happy about going home. She was anxious to show her grandmama and Barbara so many things. She said. "Ok mama, whatever you say." So, Sadie flagged down a taxicab.

As they were riding though the city, Emily said. "Look grandmama; times square is over there on the right. Look at all the beautiful Christmas trees and lights. Can we go there tomorrow, mama?"

"We will see how everyone feels in the morning before we make any plans for the day." Replied Sadie. The following day was Christmas Eve and Betty Anne and Barbara were leaving on Christmas day to go home. Betty Anne kept thinking about that train ride back to Ruby Hope. She dreaded going on the train but decided she would try to be brave about it.

She just couldn't stop thinking about what happened to Sadie and Emily when they came for thanksgiving on the train. The train slid off the tracks because of the ice and snow. She was so thankful to God for watching over her girls and keeping them safe. After breakfast Emily said she wanted to take them ice skating. Sadie asked her mother how she felt about that? "Well, I guess I can give it a try. I haven't been ice skating in over thirty years."

"Grandmama you are going to have the time of your life. And besides I will be there to help you." Sadie asked if everyone was ready to go. Barbara said she was as ready as she would ever be.

Betty Anne was a little hesitate about going but said she was willing to at least try to ice skate. This made Emily giggle as she gave her grandmama a big hug. After arriving at the ice- skating rink, Betty Anne was in aww of all the people there. She saw people that looked to be her age or older. She had just turned seventy-seven years old and wasn't sure she should be trying to ice-skate. But she didn't want to hurt Emily's feelings, so she decided she would at least try. She thought to herself, "What if I fall and break my hip or arm or even a leg. Who's going to take care of me? I guess all I can do is be as careful as I can, even though I am a bit clumsy."

After they all put on their ice skates, Emily took Betty Anne by the arm and helped her onto the ice. Sadie helped Barbara onto the ice and stayed with her until she felt comfortable ice- skating on her own. Emily held onto her grandmama and never let go of her. They had a wonderful time skating around the ice. They laughed as Betty Anne almost fail and looked like a rag doll being dragged around. Emily said. "Oh, grandmama you are so funny. I am so happy you came for Christmas. I hate for you to go home tomorrow."

The following morning Betty Anne and Barbara got up early. They had packed their bags the night before; they were ready to go to the train station. After breakfast Sadie called for a taxi to take them all to the station. They hugged and said their goodbyes as the train porter called for everyone to get aboard. He helped the two women with their luggage and advised them to hurry and get on the train. Sadie and Emily had tears in their eyes as the train disappeared down the track.

Chapter Forty-Six

It was a three-hour trip from New York to the Lancaster train station. Betty Anne and Barbara were a little nervous about the train ride. They found their seats and tried to relax for the long ride home. Betty Anne noticed two young Amish girls sitting across the aisle from them.

She spoke to them in Pennsylvania Dutch. She had picked up some of the language from Sara Jane and Levi over the years. The young girls smiled and said hullo in the same language. Betty Anne asked them if they would like to join them. The girls agreed and moved over to where they were sitting.

Betty Anne explained to them that she has been friends with an Amish couple and their family for many years. She explained she often went out to their home and spent many holidays with them. The girls were intrigued and wanted to hear more. One of the girl's name was Lilly Miller and the other one was Mary Miller. They were sisters traveling to Lancaster County from Ohio to visit their aunt and uncle. Betty Anne was surprised to hear their last names were Miller. She told them her last name was Miller also. She began to think to herself, "I wonder if my husband had some Amish roots. I think I will check into that when I get home."

Lilly and Mary said they could also speak the English language. They had been working in their father and mother's fruit market. Several Englisher's came to the market to buy produce and fruit. Their mother insisted they learn the English language so they could communicate with the customers. The four women were having a delightful time talking and laughing when suddenly two men came through the train car doors wearing mask. One of the men grabbed Lilly and told everyone to give them their money and jewelry if they didn't want anything to happen to the Amish girl.

Betty Anne could be very feisty when she wanted to and jumped up from her seat. She started toward the man who was holding onto Lilly. She said. "Who do you think you are? That girl hasn't done anything to you. Why are you holding her like that? Let her go and you will get the money. Take all our money and get out of here. Do you really think God wants you to be this way? He is watching you now and sees what you are up to. You both should be ashamed of yourselves." The man holding Lilly was surprised at Betty Anne and told her to shut up or he would hurt her. She started praying out loud for the two men and wouldn't sit down.

Both men were getting agitated with her and decided to let Lilly go back to her seat. They took everyone's money and one of the men said. "Lady I don't know who you are, but you have more guts than anybody I have ever known." Then they fled the train car. The porter was stunned at what had happened. He alerted the other porters in the other cars to watch out for the two men.

He also called the police. Lilly was crying and shaken up. Betty Anne and Barbara tried to calm her down. Lilly said. "Thank you for standing up for me. I was so afraid the man was going to shoot us."

Mary hugged Lilly and thanked Betty Anne for saving her sister. The porter asked if everyone was alright and said he couldn't stop the train because it was going so fast. He expressed regret for what had transpired and said the transport company would reimburse everyone for whatever they lost. Betty Anne and Barbara had another hour before they would be in Lancaster County. Then they would have to take a taxi to drive them to Ruby Hope Valley.

They could not wait to get home.

"I had a wonderful time in New York, Betty Anne. Thank you for asking me to go with you. I will never forget the fun we had with Sadie and Emily. I'm not sure I will ever get on another train again. This has been an experience I will never forget." Betty Anne looked over at Lilly and Mary and said to them. "I am so sorry this happened to you girls. I hope your trip home will be a better experience. I will pray for your safe travels. If you are ever in Ruby Hope Valley please come by and see us.

We would love to see you again one day. I know my Amish friends would love to meet you. We have a lovely Amish community about twenty miles outside of Ruby Hope Valley. We will be getting off the train soon and I want you know how much I enjoyed meeting you girls. Except for what happened with those two men, the trip was a lot of fun. God knows what they did, and I am sure they won't get away with their dirty dealings for very long."

As they approached the train station the women said their goodbye's. Barbara found a taxi waiting just outside of the station. The porter helped them with their luggage and again he apologized to the women. He explained to them that the two men were arrested as soon as they got off the train. The police were waiting for them. He loaded their luggage into the trunk of the taxi as they climbed inside the backseat of the car. The two women were relieved to hear the men had been arrested and Betty Anne said. *"Thanked God for your blessings on us."*

They were so happy to be heading home to Ruby Hope Valley. Betty Anne said.

"Between the train wreck two years ago, and this experience, I'm not ever going to ride this train again." Barbara agreed with her and said. "Only if there is an emergency and I have to take the train. Otherwise I don't think I want to ride on one again either."

They arrived in Ruby Hope Valley around 10 pm that night. Betty Anne was exhausted and couldn't wait to lie down. She didn't want to say anything to Barbara, but her chest had been aching all day. The situation with the train robbery made it hurt even more. She decided she would call and make an appointment with her heart doctor first thing in the morning.

Chapter Forty-Seven

The following day, Betty Anne called her doctor's office and made an appointment for herself. Her chest had been hurting her for several days, but she didn't want to spoil the trip to Sadie's, so she didn't say anything about it. She thought about Sara Jane and Levi and wondered how their Christmas turned out. She missed seeing the family and wanted to ride out to the farm.

It was still snowing and very cold outside, but she felt confident the weather would get better in a few days.

Her appointment with her heart doctor was the Friday after Christmas. She felt relieved when the snow finally stopped coming down. She wasn't a fan of driving in the wet nasty stuff but felt she didn't have any choice. She needed to find out why her chest had been bothering her.

After arriving at the doctor's office, he immediately said he wanted to take some x-rays of her chest and have some blood drawn. He listened to her heart and checked her blood pressure. After examining her, he asked her to wait in his office.

She waited with anticipation as her palms began to get sweaty. Her hands were trembling as she crossed and uncrossed her legs. Finally, after fifteen minutes the doctor came into his office. He apologized to Betty Anne for taking so long. He sat down behind his desk and took a deep breath. He said. "Betty Anne, I have been warning you for years now about your heart. I was confident the heart valve operation you had four years ago would take care of the problem, but your heart is very weak. I am concerned that if you don't slow down, you could have a heart attack. We will see how the blood work and the x-ray turns out and let you know.

On the ride home from the doctor's office, she began thinking about her life. "I love volunteering at the orphanage: and I don't want to give it up. I love finding homes for those kids and being there for them. I guess there comes a time in one's life that we must except the fact that we aren't getting any younger." Tears began to swell up in her eyes as she drove home from the doctor's office. She decided she wouldn't say anything to anyone. She would keep her health problems to herself. But she would slow down and try to take better care of herself. Afterall, I do have a lot to look forward to; I want to be here for all those who count on me.

She said a silent prayer thanking God for all his blessings. She asked him to give her the strength she needed to get through each day and to be there for her friends and family.

The days that followed seemed so gloomy and cold outside. The snow had finally diminished, and the days seemed to be getting clearer. Each day seemed colder than the day before. She thought, "Maybe it's just me, I seem to be cold all the time." She didn't feel like going outside and decided to just stay home until the weather got better. She knew Sara Jane would be worried about her, but she didn't have any way of getting in touch with her. She thought maybe Levi and Sara Jane would come to town when the weather warmed up and check on her.

January and February were harsh months in Pennsylvania, and most people just stayed inside their homes. The cold weather and snow had just about crippled the whole county. Sadie had given her mother a laptop for Christmas and she decided she would try to get it hooked up to Wi-Fi. She tried calling the cable company several times but was unable to get through to them. This was mainly because of the weather. She wanted to do some research on her husband's family. With the name Miller she just knew he could have been Amish.

She thought about him for a while as she relaxed in her recliner. She thought, "well let's see now. He was born and raised right here in Ruby Hope Valley and he never spoke much about his mother and father. Wouldn't that be something if Sadie had Amish roots. I wonder what Sadie would think about that, as she fail asleep." Sara Jane was concerned about Betty Anne and said to Levi one day. "As soon as this weather gets better, I want to go into Ruby Hope and see if Betty Anne is doing ok."

At last February came to an end and the snow stopped falling. It began to melt on the streets as it gave people a chance to get out of their homes to go shopping. Flowers began to show their little heads as they popped up out of the ground. Even though the weather was still cold and windy outside; everyone bundled up and went about their business. Betty Anne decided she would cut back on her hours at the foster home. She had worked hard all year long and it was time to let Barbara take over for her. She called her friend and neighbor to come over when she had time. She wanted to discuss the foster home with her.

The following afternoon, Barbara decided to give Betty Anne a visit. They sat down at the kitchen table while drinking a hot cup of coffee. Betty Anne had made some delicious cinnamon rolls and offered one to Barbara. They sat for a while just talking of ordinary things such as the weather and their trip to New York. Betty Anne began to tell her friend she wanted to cut back on her hours at the foster home.

"Barbara, I know how you love volunteering at the foster home, and I wanted to see if you would be interested in working more days. I think it's time for me to cutback, but I want to be sure there is someone like you to take over for me. I don't want to leave the children with no one to help them find homes. Barbara knew in her heart Betty Anne was getting up in age and was having some problems with her heart again. Barbara said. "You know you can count on me, Betty Anne. I would love to be an advocate for the children. I will work hard for them, after all I have had a good teacher."

"You have been a wonderful supporter for these kids through the years, Betty Anne and I won't let you down."

"I trust you to do what is right for the children and so I am not worried. I still want to go there at least two days a week for a little while longer. But I need you to fight for them and give them hope for a better future." Barbara said she could count on her and thanked her for having so much confidence in her. Betty Anne continued to spend time at the foster home for a while, then she stopped going all together. Thus, ending her days as a volunteer.

Chapter Forty-Eight

Joseph Levi and Betsy had their wedding set for April 5th, 2003. Sara Jane glanced at the calendar and read the date of springs first arrival. It was supposed to arrive around March 20th. She was doubtful. The snow would probably return a few times before that would happen.

Even though the fields were beginning to turn green and there were signs that spring was pushing its way across the landscape, March had come roaring in like a blast of cold air. Sara Jane said. "Winter conditions have been wet, and the grounds have been so frozen, I guess the birds are happy to see a little warm weather." Joseph Levi couldn't wait to get started on the house. As soon as he left work each day, he would ride out to his property in the enclosed carriage. It seemed like old Ralph already knew the way. As soon as he climbed inside the carriage he would say, "Ok old Ralph, let's go." And the horse would head straight to the apple orchard. Old Ralph would draw in the air through his nostrils to see if he could detect any apples. Joseph Levi would say to him, "Now old Ralph, you know the apples won't grow until summer, but don't worry I brought you a couple."

As the days began to get longer, Joseph Levi would go out to the property and nail a few boards up on the house. Some of the Amish men in the community would meet him there and help him with the framing and roof. It was going to be a small house at first with only two bedrooms, a living room and kitchen. He decided no matter what it cost he wanted to have indoor plumbing for Becky. Most of the people in his community had outdoor facilities, but since working at the animal clinic, he had gotten used to the indoor restroom.

The weather remained cold, wet and unpredictable. Joseph Levi wanted to get as much done to the house as he could before the wedding in April. It was still early March, but the weather conditions just didn't want to corporate. It made it difficult to work on the house. The men worked hard and never let on how cold it was. Some days it snowed and other days it rained. But they always showed up and worked hard until it got so dark they couldn't see any more. The men would light lanterns and hold them out the window of their carriages so they could see the roads. Joseph Levi thanked the men over and over for helping him in such weather.

By the end of March, the roof was on and the walls were up. Joseph Levi and Betsy's home was almost finished. The plumbing had not been installed yet, so the men built a little privy out back of the house. He said to Betsy one day as they were walking around the house. "I promised I would have you an indoor restroom, Betsy; and you will have it. I must find the right people to install it."

"I'm not worried, Joseph Levi, I know you are doing your best. The weather has been so unpleasant, I don't know how you got this much done."

"If it wasn't for the other men, all this may not have gotten done. They worked so hard in the cold and rain.

I am so amazed at how thoughtful they are." Betsy agreed with him and said. "I'm so happy Joseph Levi. Just think our wedding is only a week away. Mother said we could stay with her until the house is finished. Is that ok with you Joseph?" I'm happy if you are happy. He didn't mind staying at her house until their home was finished. He liked her mother and knew she needed someone to stay with her and her little brother for a while. James said he wanted a little dog, so Joseph Levi was determined to find him one.

Joseph Levi knew Betsy would want to take Bobo and Chloe with her when they moved into their new home. There were always strays brought into the clinic; so, he shouldn't have a problem finding James a dog. Afterall, that is how he got Maggie a few years ago. He loved Maggie and wished he could take her with him, but the other kids wanted her to stay at the farm. Samuel John would look after her, so he wasn't worried. Betsy said. "I really hate to take Bobo and Chloe away from James when we get married; but I would be lost without them."

"Don't you worry about that Betsy; I'm going to find him a nice little dog of his own."

One afternoon Betty Anne decided to drive out to the farm. The weather was still a little damp but seemed to be getting warmer. On her way she noticed a little white dog walking on the side of the road. She stopped her car and called to the dog. He was friendly and came to her immediately. She spoke to him as if he was a child. "What in the world are you doing out here on this road all along. You don't have a tag on, so I guess you are a stray.

Come on boy, I know someone that will take good care of you." She picked him up and put him in the backseat of her car as she headed down the road to Sara Jane's farm.

Bosco

Chapter Forty-Nine

Joseph Levi took the dog Betty Anne found on the side of the road. He examined him at the clinic and decided to name him Bosco. He thought to himself, "Bosco would be perfect for Betsy's little brother, James." Bosco was in good health, but a little under nourished. "I believe after he fills out some and gets all his shots, he will be a good dog. Come on boy, lets get you all fixed up for James. He is going to love you and take good care of you." After Bosco had been evaluated and had all his shots, he decided to take him to James. The boy was excited to get the little white dog. He hugged him and whispered in his ear. "I love you Bosco."

The days were beginning to get longer, and the rain had stopped coming down at last.

The wedding was just a few days away and Sara Jane was getting nervous and anxious. Hannah and Betty Anne had been a big help to her during the past couple of months. She had baked several pies and had started on the wedding cake. She would still need to frost and decorate the cake but seemed to have everything under control. Joseph Levi and Betsy decided to have the wedding in the apple orchard.

Sara Jane was a little disappointed because she was planning to have it at the farm. The orchard was a beautiful place where the flowers were beginning to bloom despite the cool weather. Levi and Samuel had setup chairs and tables for everyone. The women in the quilting group had made beautiful lavender ribbons and placed them on each chair. The Amish men in the community had constructed a small gazebo for the couple to get married in. It stood just out of site of the little white house.

Betsy had picked the color lavender for her dress and thought it would be beautiful for this time of the year. All the bridesmaid's dresses would be lavender as well. The best men would wear lavender shirts under their black suits. This was the custom of the Amish people.

Betsy had asked Daisy and Cindy to be her brides' maids, too. The girls were excited to be in the wedding and hugged and thanked Betsy for asking them. Sara Jane had been working night and day on the dresses; as well as the wedding. She was so tired but knew it was all for her special son, Joseph Levi.

If she had not had help from Betty Anne and Betsy's mother, Hannah, she couldn't imagine what she would have done. This was going to be one of the biggest and most beautiful weddings the Amish community had ever had. Everyone loved Joseph Levi and wanted to see him get married. The apple orchard was the perfect place for their wedding. Joseph Levi had almost finished their house except for the plumbing and cabinets in the small kitchen. The little white house stood there in the distance as the marriage took place.

Sara Jane couldn't help but remember Joseph Levi as a little boy as the Bishop spoke to them in Pennsylvania Dutch. The tears began to roll down her cheeks as she held onto Levi. He put his arms around her as tears began to swell up in his eyes. The couple looked so lovely standing there in the gazebo in front of the Bishop. After the wedding, everyone huddled around the couple and gave them their best wishes. Joseph Levi was all smiles as he ran over and gave his mama and dad a hug. He said. "Mama, dad this is the happiest day of my life."

Levi and Sara Jane hugged their son and told him how much they loved him and how happy they were for him and Betsy. Betty Anne ran over and gave Joseph Levi and Betsy a big hug as tears were falling down her cheeks. She then walked over and embraced Sara Jane. The two women were so happy for Joseph Levi. Betty Anne said to Sara Jane. "That boy has always been so special to me. I will never forget what he had to go through as a child. Just look at him now. So tall and handsome and proud. I love him as if he were my very own."

After everyone had eaten a delicious meal of fried chicken, corn on the cob, mac and cheese and all kinds of casseroles, they began to help clean off the tables. The men folks folded all the chairs and loaded them into the back of Levi's wagon. The sky suddenly opened, and the rains came down in buckets. The women and children ran to their carriages as the men ran behind them. The family, which included Betty Anne, ran up onto the front porch of the little white house. Betty Anne said.

"My what an exciting day this has been. I was afraid this might happen. The weatherman forecast rain, but I didn't want to believe it would happen on this day of all days."

The rain lasted for thirty minutes and then the sunshine came out. Sara Jane said. "Thank goodness we were able to get the food put away before the rains started." The women laughed and finished loading up their carriages. After a while, only the family were left in the orchard.

Joseph Levi and Betsy took Hannah and James home. Betsy said to Joseph Levi. "I think we should keep the gazebo in the orchard. It's so beautiful and it will always remind us of our wedding day." Joseph Levi replied, "That's a great idea Betsy. We won't dissemble it but keep it the way it is. I will put a nice coat of white paint on it, too."

"Oh Levi, that sounds so nice."

As the days passed, Joseph Levi and Betsy continued to live with her mother and little brother, James. After work each day, the couple would meet at the new house. Joseph Levi would paint while Betsy cleaned the floors and kitchen. As time went by, they began to move furniture into the house. Her mother, Hannah, gave her several plates, cups and a few pots and pans. Each day, Betsy would take a few more items with her to the house.

The kitchen cabinets were finished and looked beautiful. They were made of solid wood, and Joseph Levi had stained them with a lovely oak finish. Betsy had a hope chest which she had stored several items over the past two years. Several of the Amish women had given her quits and sheets and a few dollies and three pillows which she would use on the beds.

The couple had also visited the flea market several times and purchased a small table and four chairs for the kitchen. They also purchased a sofa and one chair.

Betsy had a big oak bed her father had made her when she was a small child which she wanted to put in the house. A neighbor, Mr. Miller was a good plumber and had put plumbing in his house, so Joseph Levi asked for his help. The Amish gentleman was happy to help him with the plumbing job. Joseph Levi and Mr. Miller worked hard side by side every afternoon. It took a couple of weeks to get it all installed. By mid-July they were ready to move.

Betsy was excited and couldn't wait to move into the little white house in the orchard.

By the end of April, the orchard was lit up with all kinds and flowers. The apple trees had begun to bloom with their lovely white flower. The apples would not start to grow until June, but the orchard was ablaze with color. Betsy would stand on the front porch and stair at all the beauty around her home. She knew in her heart they had made the right decision to build their home in the apple orchard.

An Apple poem by Margaret Hillart
Apple Magic
In every single apple lies
A truly magical surprise,
Instead of slicing down, slice through
And watch the star appear for you

Chapter Fifty

Joseph Levi and Betsy were so happy living in their little house. Betsy had made a real home for them. Joseph Levi couldn't wait to get home every day after work. He would play with Bobo and Chloe in the orchard until dinner was ready. One evening at dinner, he said. "Betsy, what do you think about a small barn where we can keep the horse and carriage? I hate keeping old Ralph tied up outside all the time. When the weather gets cold, old Ralph would have a place to stay warm."

"That would be wonderful. It's such a beautiful place with all the apple trees and flowers blooming. I hate to see winter coming."

As the days began to creep into fall, Joseph Levi decided to ask some of the Amish gentlemen to help him build a barn. Early one morning in September, Joseph Levi and Betsy woke up to a loud clatter. As he looked out the bedroom window, he noticed several carriages.

His Amish neighbors had already started building the barn. He put on his pants and shirt and grabbed his straw hat and ran out the door. He was happy to see all these men and joined in with them as they began to raise the barn. He was amazed at how efficient and fast these men worked.

In the meantime, Betsy had started making coffee and muffins for all of them. She carried the coffee pot and a platter full of blueberry muffins out to the men working on the barn.

They were all delighted to see her coming and stopped what they were doing. Joseph Levi motioned for them to come over and have some refreshments. After the men had eaten, they proceeded to go back to work on the barn. It only took a couple of days and the barn was finished. Joseph Levi was so grateful to all his neighbors and couldn't thank them enough.

He said to the men. "Old Ralph will be so happy to have a roof over his head when the weather gets cold." The men laughed as they walked to their buggies to go home. They all thanked Betsy for the coffee and muffins and waved goodbye as one buggy after another drove up the dirt road. The couple stood there looking at their new barn. Joseph Levi said. "Mr. Miller and his son, Leroy said they would come back next weekend and help me paint the barn. I think I will paint it red. What do you think Betsy?" She replied. "A red barn is perfect, Joseph Levi. Then we can get some pine straw to cover the floor. Old Ralph will be happy with his new home."

The fall season was beautiful with all the pumpkins everywhere. The stores in the town of Ruby Hope were lovely with their front windows all decorated with the fall colors. Levi and Sara Jane's fields were overflowing with pumpkins. Samuel and Jacob worked hard loading them up for the market. Sara Jane decorated her front porch with several pumpkins and decided to take a few over to Joseph Levi and Betsy. The couple were delighted to get the pumpkins and decided to place a few on their new porch. Betsy thanked Sara Jane and said. "I think this orchard is the most beautiful place in the whole Amish community."

As the seasons passed, Thanksgiving was approaching. Sara Jane and Levi were getting prepared for the whole family to arrive for the holiday. Betty Anne bought a turkey and decided to take it to Sara Jane. The weather was beginning to get very cold in Pennsylvania. Betty Anne began thinking how unpredictable the weather was all the time. She thought to herself, "I sure hope it doesn't start snowing until after Thanksgiving. I really want to be able to come out here and be with this family."

The weather continued to get colder and colder, but Betty Anne was happy the snow had not begun yet. It was Thanksgiving morning as she prepared to ride out to the farm for the day.

She put her boots on and a heavy coat. She knew Sara Janes home wasn't warmed by central heat but only by a big fireplace. So, she decided to wear her new heavy sweater she had bought in New York. As she drove down the dirt roads that led to the farm, she noticed how the green fields had started to turn brown. They were so beautiful in the summer and fall and now they lay dormant just waiting for the snow to come as it always did in the winter.

As Betty Anne approached the farm, she noticed all the horse and carriages parked down by the barn. She thought to herself, "My goodness how this family has grown. I am so lucky to be a part of it." She said a silent prayer while sitting in her car. *Dear Lord, please bless this family and keep all of them safe. Thank you, Lord, for letting me be with them another year and sharing this special day."*

While enjoying this wonderful feast Sara Jane had put on the table, Jacob said he had something to share. Everyone got quiet as Levi said. "What is it Jacob, don't keep us in suspense." Jacob looked over at Grace and smiled. "Well, everyone, Grace and I are going to have a baby." Everyone began to clap and raise their voices in excitement. Sara Jane and Levi jumped up out of their seats and embraced Jacob and Grace. Sara Jane said. "Oh Jacob, I am so happy for you and Grace. I'm going to knit a beautiful quilt for my new grandbaby."

Grace said. "You have plenty of time Sara Jane, the baby isn't due until April of next year."

Betty Anne started thinking about the day as she drove home that afternoon. She thought to herself, "What a wonderful day this has been. I am so proud and happy for Jacob. I wonder where this boy would be if he had not come to the farm to live. *Lord only you know the answer to that. Thank you for bringing Jacob into our lives."*

Chapter Fifty-One

Joseph Levi and Betsy started to prepare for their first Christmas in their new home.

Betsy couldn't wait to decorate the house. The Amish were not allowed to have Christmas trees, but could hang wreaths on their front doors: and Christmas cards around the house. Betsy wanted her new home to be as festive as she could make it. She loved to bake like her mother and Sara Jane but the weather prevented her from getting out to the store. Snow had finally arrived in Ruby Hope Valley. She decided she would ask Joseph Levi to stop by the local Amish store and pick up a few things she needed.

It was a slow week at the clinic because of the cold weather and snow. Joseph Levi decided to leave work early one afternoon so he could shop for Betsy. The local Amish grocery store was located near the clinic. Old Ralph had a hard time pulling the carriage but managed. Joseph Levi had put a blanket over the old horse and hoped it would help keep him warm. He held the reins and coaxed the horse to go forward. All he could hear was the clip clopping of old Ralph's hooves in the snow.

He thought about the orchard and couldn't wait for the flowers to start blooming again. It was a beautiful place and the best part about it was Betsy was there. Betsy had a long list of items she needed from the store for him to get. He knew the store may close early because of the bad weather, so he hurried to get there in time. Old Ralph came through for him and made it just in time.

The store owner welcomed him inside and said he was about to close. "You just made it Joseph Levi. Go ahead and get what you need, I don't mind waiting for you."

"Thank you, Mr. Miller, Betsy would be mad at me if I didn't bring the baking supplies she wants home today." Mr. Miller replied. "I know what you mean, son. These Amish women love to bake. My wife is always baking something delicious." Joseph Levi and old Ralph made it home with all the baking supplies Betsy wanted that day.

Betsy was so happy and proud of him for getting everything she needed. She had cooked a pot of stew for dinner and he could hardly wait to eat. "I'm starving Betsy, when are we going to have dinner?" The two of them sat down to dinner as Joseph Levi begun to say the blessing. *"Lord, thank you for this wonderful food Betsy has prepared for us today. Thank you for all the blessings you have bestowed upon us. Amen."*

"This is the best beef stew I have ever eaten, Betsy. Where did you learn to cook like this?"

"Oh, mother started teaching me how to cook when I was just ten years old."

Joseph Levi was proud of Betsy for her wonderful cooking. "You know us Amish girls learn to cook and clean house at an early age. Why I bet Cindy already knows how to cook?"

"Yes, she does as a matter of fact. Mama started teaching her early too. Cindy is going to make some Amish boy a good wife one of these days. She loves to help mama around the house, too. I don't know about Daisy. She's a mama's girl; so, we will have to wait and see what she becomes." The couple enjoyed the stew as they laughed and talked about their families.

Sara Jane knew there would be a lot of people for Christmas dinner this year. She started her baking early and decided she would bake a Christmas cake this year. She would put green and red icing around the cake along with colorful sprinkles over the top of it. The family would love it. Once again, this year she would have to figure out the sitting arrangements. She thought to herself, "This family sure is growing. If this keeps up, we will need to buy a bigger table."

After dinner that evening, she sat down with Levi and asked if they could take a trip to the big flea market. "I think we should buy a bigger table before Christmas dinner. Our family is growing so much; I don't think this old table is going to be big enough." Levi replied, "I think you are right." So, they decided they would wait and make the trip as soon as the weather cleared up.

Sara Jane was looking forward to Christmas; she had a new daughter in law in the family and a new grandbaby on the way in the spring. She couldn't be more pleased. The family arrived on Christmas day as usual. This year they would have Joseph Levi, Betsy, Jacob and Grace. Also, Samuel and Mattie Sue and their sons, Ethan Nathaniel and Joey. Betty Anne was going to try her best to be there. She was getting up in age now and the ride out to the farm was beginning to tire her. The snow wasn't much help either. Sara Jane's dad and brother would also be there.

Everyone arrived in their enclosed carriages without any problems with the weather. All except Betty Anne. Sara Jane begin to worry about her and decided to send Cindy down to the outdoor phone booth, to call her. Betty Anne told Cindy how sorry she was, but she wasn't going to be able to make it to Christmas dinner this year. She said. "Cindy, please tell Sara Jane and Levi I'm not feeling well today, and the weather is too bad for me to drive in." Cindy replied.

"We will miss you grandmama and we will say a special prayer for you to get better."

Betty Anne felt bad about not going to Sara Jane's Christmas dinner. But in her heart, she knew the time had come for her to slow down even more. Sara Jane was disappointed and worried about Betty Anne. She said to Levi." I wish there was something we could do for her."

"The Lord will provide a way for Betty Anne and only he knows what we should do for her." Be patient Sara Jane, the answer will come to us."

While the family enjoyed a delicious dinner that Sara Jane had prepared, two announcements were made. Ethan Nathaniel spoke up and said he was going to start working in the blacksmith shop with his dad, Samuel. He said. "I'm almost eleven years old now and I want to learn the trade." Samuel was all smiles and said. "Ethan is ready to learn the trade and I am proud he wants to learn from me." Joseph Levi said. "That is great news Ethan, I think you will be a good blacksmith. Dad when you retire you will have three good men running the shop."

After a while, Joseph Levi spoke again. "I have some news to share with all of you today, too. Betsy and I are expecting a baby in the fall." Sara Jane and Levi were delighted to hear the news of another grandbaby. Sara Jane said. "What a blessed day this has been. Two grandbabies in one year. Now I know I'm getting old."

Chapter Fifty-Two

Christmas was over and it was time to celebrate a new year. The Miller family decided to have church at their home the following week. Sara Jane and Levi couldn't wait to tell their neighbors about the new grandbabies they were having. Of course, in the Amish community word gets around fast, so most of the people already new about the wonderful news for the Click family. The weather was bitter cold, and snow was still on the ground. The horses had a hard time pulling the enclosed carriages, but the people of the Amish valley managed to go to church no matter what. They would bundle up and put blankets across everyone's laps inside the carriages.

The Millers had benches sat up in their living room which was larger than most of the Amish homes. They would have a big fireplace full of wood going to warm everyone as they filed into the room. The Bishop would start the service with a prayer for all the people. Then they would sing from the Amish Himmel. After the Bishop gave his sermon the men would line the benches against the wall. Then the women would set up a long table with all kinds of casseroles, pies and cakes.

The women folks couldn't stop talking to Sara Jane about her new grandbabies that were on the way. They seemed so happy for them as Mattie Sue said.

"We will have to make two quilts for the babies. When shall we get started?" Sara Jane said.

"One of the babies is due in April, so why don't we wait until the weather gets better. The quilting group could meet in March and still have time to finish the quilt." The women agreed that would be the best. They were all excited and anxious to get started.

After arriving home from church, Sara Jane began to go through her old hope chest. She had been storing away old pieces of material for years. She knew in her heart this day would come and she wanted to be prepared. She couldn't wait to get started on her grandbaby's quilts.

She sat down on the floor and started taking the pieces out of the chest. As she looked at each one she began to reminisce about her two sons when they were little. She picked up a piece of green quilting that came from Samuel John's old baby quilt. She held it to her chest as tears began to fall down her cheeks.

As she picked up the material she had saved, she closed her eyes and said a little prayer.

"Lord, bless this quilting material and bless the babies who will be wrapped up in it." Sara Jane suddenly felt a peacefulness come over her as she continued to sit on the floor and go through the hope chest. She came upon the dollies her mother had made for her before she got married to Levi. She thought to herself, "I haven't looked in this hope chest for a long time. There are so many memories stored away in here. I think I will give these to Cindy to keep for her home one day. I need to talk to Levi about building Cindy a hope chest of her own."

Cindy was fifteen now and had been keeping things in a big old brown box in the corner of her room. She had kept all her old aprons and kappa's in there along with the Amish bible. Sara Jane had made her several pillowcases and sheets for her bed. So, she kept them folded neatly away in the big old brown box. In the bottom of the box hidden way from everyone was a little doll. This was all she had left from her past life; she wasn't sure why she kept it. Maybe to remind her of how lucky she was to find Sara Jane and Levi.

Sara Jane was eager for the weather to get better. She wanted to go into Ruby Hope Valley and check on Betty Anne. The family missed seeing her Christmas and she was worried about her. Betty Anne was getting up in age and couldn't drive out to the farm the way she used to. She asked Cindy if she would bundle up and walk down to the outdoor phone booth for her.

She wanted her to call Betty Anne and see how she was doing.

Sara Jane was anxious for Cindy to come back and let her know how her friend was.

Betty Anne was happy to hear from Cindy and said. "Tell Sara Jane and Levi how sorry I am I missed Christmas with all of you. I can't drive the car in this awful weather anymore. Tell your mama I am doing ok. I have had a little cold but other than that I am fine."

"Mama can't wait to see you; we missed you this year. She plans to come to Ruby Hope as soon as the weather lets up."

"Tell Sara Jane, Barbara comes over to check on me almost every day. She even brings me meals from time to time."

"Ok, I will, grandmama. We love you and miss you."

The long cold days of winter seemed to go by slowly. Sara Jane said to Levi after dinner one evening. "Levi, as soon as it warms up would you start building Cindy a hope chest. She keeps all her belongings in an old box in the corner of her bedroom."

"Yes, I would be happy to build her a hope chest and I may even build little Daisy one too."

"That would be wonderful Levi. I know the girls will be excited to have their own hope chest."

Finally, the snow began to melt away, and the birds started to sing their beautiful songs.

Sara Jane was so happy to see the sunshine and hear the birds outside the kitchen window sing.

She was anxious to get started on the grandbaby's quilt and she wanted to go into town to see Betty Anne. She thought to herself, "Now that spring is here I have so much I want to do. But the first thing is to go into Ruby Hope and see Betty Anne."

Chapter Fifty-Three

Spring had finally come to Ruby Hope Valley. The birds were singing their lovely songs and the grass in the fields had begun to turn green. Jacob and Grace's baby was due anytime now. The couple had an Amish midwife that came around each day to check on her. Sara Jane and Grace's mother, Martha Fisher were always hovering over Grace. They couldn't understand why they were not the ones taking care of her instead of a midwife. Levi reminded Sara Jane that Betty Anne was the same way when she was expecting Joseph Levi and Samuel John. "Be patient and let the midwife take care of Grace. You will have plenty of time with the baby later."

Sara Jane decided Levi was right and stayed away until the baby was born. It was three o'clock in the afternoon and the midwife had just arrived. She noticed Grace wasn't feeling well and asked her if she could do anything for her. Grace said. "I'm having a lot of pain in my back."

The midwife immediately asked Jacob to boil some hot water and to give her some extra sheets and a blanket. She told Jacob it was time for the baby to come. Lucy, the midwife delivered the baby boy without any problems. She wrapped him in a blanket and handed him to Jacob. "He is a healthy little thing and with big lungs. Just listen to him cry."

Jacob held his little son and couldn't stop smiling. He asked Lucy if she would stop by the farm and let his mama and dad know the baby had arrived. Grace and Jacob were undecided about the baby's name. They wanted him to have a strong Amish name that would carry him through his life with respect and honor. Levi and Sara Jane arrived soon after and were so excited about the baby. Sara Jane asked Grace how she was feeling and told her that her mother was on her way to see her and the baby.

It didn't take long before the whole family had arrived to see the baby. Jacob said. "Grace and I are not sure what we want to name our son. We are thinking about the name Mervin. What do you and dad think about that name mama?" Levi and Sara Jane said they thought that was a fine Amish name. Jacob and Grace decided they would call their son, Mervin Joseph Click.

After everyone had seen the baby it was time to leave the couple with their new son. Mervin was a good baby and slept most of the time. The midwife, Lucy continued to come by to check on mother and baby for several days after the delivery. "Grace and the baby are doing just fine, and she should be up and around in no time." In the meantime, Sara Jane came over almost every day to help with the meals. She loved to sit in the living room rocking chair and rock Mervin. She was so proud and couldn't wait for Betty Anne to see her new grandson.

Betty Anne began to feel stronger as the days went by. She asked Barbara if she would drive her out to the farm. She couldn't wait to see Jacob's new son and the family. Barbara said.

"Of course, Betty Anne, when did you want to go?"

"Would tomorrow be too soon, Barbara?"

"Tomorrow it is. I will pick you up at 11:00." As they rode out to the farm, Betty Anne said.

"This Amish countryside is so beautiful. I have always loved my drive out to the farm. Now I am getting so old and feeble I must have someone else take me. Oh, how I long for days passed."

I have been coming out to Amish country for over twenty years now. I have so many memories tucked away in my mind and heart. Those memories are what keeps me going every day. I do wish I could turn back time." As soon as Barbara drove up the dirt road to the farm Betty Anne had tears swell up in her eyes. Barbara looked over at her and asked if she was ok? "Yes, I'm fine, I just get a little emotional when I come down this road. It holds so many memories for me."

"I know it does Betty Anne. You know our memories are what keeps us going."

Betty Anne said. "I just love this family so much and their way of living has inspired me.

I don't know for the life of me how they have allowed me to be a part of their lives all these years."

"Betty Anne, you have been an inspiration to them, and they owe you so much. They owe you their love and respect and treat you just like one of them. And you respect them and their culture. So, I would say it's a two-way road. Love, respect and inspiration on both sides.

You are their family and always will be a part of them."

"Yes, I know you are right Barbara. And without a friend like you, I don't know what I would have done all these years. You are my closest friend and I love you. I want you to know that." Barbara reached over and laid her hand on Betty Anne's hands and said to her. "I love you too, Miss Betty Anne, and don't you forget it." They both laughed and had tears in their eyes at the same time.

Chapter Fifty-Four

As they pulled up into the yard, Sara Jane came to the front door and looked out. When she saw Betty Anne; she ran down the steps and opened the door of the car for her. She grabbed her and hugged her and said. "Oh, I am so happy to see you. I was going to come see you as soon as I could, but I have been so busy helping Grace with the new baby. But you are here now and that's all that matters." Betty Anne said. "I can't wait to see the baby. I brought them a little gift too. I hope they will like it."

"You and Barbara come on in the house and have a nice cup of hot tea and a slice of Rhubarb Pie. I just made it this morning."

The three women sat down at the kitchen table as Sara Jane poured them a cup of tea.

"How are things going at the orphanage Barbara?"

"Oh, they are great. Everyone misses Betty Anne of course. The children ask about her almost every day."

"Well, in my opinion, that place should be called the Betty Anne home for children. She put her life into finding homes for those kids. And just look at Jacob now. A wonderful son, husband father and a great blacksmith.

Levi and I are so proud of him. If it wasn't for Betty Anne, we would have never even known about him and his two sisters. We love them as if I had given birth to them."

Betty Anne said. "By the way, when do I get to see little Mervin?"

"As soon as you finish your pie." They laughed and continued to talk about the children. "I can't wait for you to see Cindy and Daisy. They have grown so much in the past few months. Cindy has turned out to be a beautiful young woman. There is a young Amish boy named Eli Lapp interested in her, but she doesn't seem to be interested in him at all. Samuel John has fallen for a girl named Linda. He goes to the singings on Saturday nights and meets with her. I am afraid he is getting too involved. He's only seventeen now and way too young to get married."

Sara Jane continued to talk about Linda and Samuel John. She is a nice girl and doesn't mind him walking with a cane, but I'm not ready for him to leave home just yet." Betty Anne and Barbara agreed with Sara Jane. They both thought Samuel John was too young to be getting married. "What does he say about all this?"

"He says they are just friends and I shouldn't worry about such things. But I am worried. I have been praying on it and I decided to leave it in God's hands. He knows what's best for Samuel John."

"I think that is the right thing to do Sara Jane, replied Betty Anne.

After they had eaten their pie, Sara Jane asked them if they were ready to go see the baby?" Betty Anne said she wanted to stop by the shop and see Jacob before going to see Mervin. As they approached the shop, Jacob came out to get in his buggy. He was going home for lunch and was happy to see the women. "Come follow me in my buggy and I will take y'all to see the baby." Barbara and Betty Anne followed behind him in the car. Grace was feeding the baby as they came in. She asked Betty Anne if she would like to hold Mervin? She sat down in the rocking chair and rocked the baby for a while. He slept in her arms as she cuddled him.

While the baby slept in Betty Anne's arms, Grace made them a cup of tea. She had baked a loaf of fresh bread that morning and had also cooked a pot of vegetable soup for Jacob's lunch. She offered the women lunch, but they declined, saying they just had a slice of Sara Jane's rhubarb pie. Betty Anne said. "Yall go ahead and have your lunch. I am perfectly satisfied sitting here holding this beautiful baby." They all laughed at her while she rocked back and forth in the rocking chair.

Betty Anne asked Barbara to bring in the gifts for Jacob and Grace. She had bought a blue baby blanket with a satin edge to it. She had also brought the couple a basket of fruit. Betty Anne knew the Amish didn't like to accept gifts except on special occasions. Jacob and Grace were very pleased with the gifts; as they hugged Betty Anne and Barbara and thanked them.

He kissed the baby on his head and left to go back to work. Grace took the baby from Betty Anne and placed him in his little crib. She then placed the blue blanket over him. Betty Anne was pleased as she smiled down at Mervin.

As Barbara and Betty Anne drove through the countryside, they reflected on the day.

Betty Anne said. "I am still amazed at how fine Jacob and his sisters have turned out. You would never know they were adopted."

"I think you found them a good home just in time. They were at the age they needed guidance and love in their lives. And you gave them that. Just like you have given all those children at the home through the years."

You should be commended on all your good works, Betty Anne."

"Oh no, I did what I could do for those kids because I loved each one of them. I felt like they needed to have a good home with people who would take good care of them and love them. I didn't do it out of any selfish means or recognition for myself."

"I know you didn't, but you still need to know how much you are respected and loved by all those people that adopted the children. And I am sure those kids would love to tell you how grateful they are." They drove the rest of the way home in silence.

All along, Barbara was thinking of how she was going to get the towns people to honor Betty Anne for all the good works she had done over the past twenty years. She began to think to herself, "I know, I will go to talk to the town Mayor and Solicitor. They would be happy to honor Betty Anne.

Chapter Fifty-Five

Spring and summer were coming to an end. The flowers in the apple orchard were still blooming. Colors blazed across the beautiful field as Betsy looked out her kitchen window. It would be fall soon and the baby would be here. She could hardly wait. Sara Jane was anxious for her grandbaby to be born. Betsy had gotten so big; she was miserable and could hardly get around anymore. "Mama, I am really worried about Betsy. Would you mind checking on her when you have time?"

In the back of his mind, he was always thinking about the baby having kidney problems like he did. He thought to himself, "What if our baby has to go through what I did when I was little boy." As he drove the carriage home one afternoon, he said a silent prayer for his baby to be. *"Dear Lord, please don't let my little son or daughter have any kidney problems or any kind of sickness when it's born. I don't want my Betsy to have to go through what my mama had to go through with me. Thank you, Lord, for giving me the life I always wanted and keeping me well all these years. I pray for continued good health for myself and my family. Amen."*

As the days got closer for Betsy to give birth to her baby, Sara Jane decided she wanted to be the midwife for Betsy. She began to think to herself, "I know how's it done and most of the Amish women have their babies on their own with just a little help from a midwife. I can be Betsy's midwife and help her through this." She sat down with Levi one evening after dinner and asked him what he thought about her being Betsy's midwife?"

"Sara Jane, what if something happened and you didn't know what to do. I don't think you should involve yourself in that."

She was disappointed with his response as tears began to swell up in her eyes. "But Levi, I want to be involved as much as I can. But I guess you are right, something could happen, and I wouldn't know what to do. I will tell Joseph Levi to get one of the local midwifes to come and take care of Betsy. Maybe I could assist her in some way."

Joseph Levi asked one of the local midwives to come over and watch after Betsy for several days as the time got nearer. The baby was due anytime now and he didn't want her to be home alone. Sara Jane came over to see about her every day. She prepared their meals for them, to keep Betsy from having to be on her feet. Joseph Levi spoke with Jim Peterson about taking some time off from the clinic. "I really need to be home with Betsy when the baby comes, and I would like to take a few days off. I hope it won't inconvenience you."

Jim was happy to give Joseph Levi some time off. "Joseph Levi you have never taken any time off and you work so hard. Of course, you can take as much time as you need. Keep me updated on the delivery, would you?" He was thankful to Jim and said he would send word to him as soon as the baby arrived.

It was three o'clock in the morning when Betsy reached over and woke Joseph Levi up.

"I think my water has broken. I believe it's time for this little fellow to say hello to the world."

"Oh Betsy, I will go wake the midwife up. You stay still and don't get up." He ran downstairs and woke Ruby up and told her Betsy's water had broken. She jumped up and ran upstairs to check on Betsy. She said to Joseph Levi. "She's in labor and I need you to go boil some hot water for me. And bring me several towels, sheets and a fresh gown for Betsy."

He ran to the kitchen and put the water on the wood burning stove to boil. Then he ran back upstairs and got towels sheets and a gown for Betsy. He was completely out of breath. He was so excited and wished he had a way to let his mama and dad know the baby was coming. He would just have to wait until morning to let them know.

In the next few minutes, Ruby said. "Here it comes Mr. Click. It's a beautiful baby girl.

Here, take the baby and wrap her up in those clean towels until I can bath her. Betsy began to squirm and cry. She was having a lot of pain. Ruby wasn't sure what was happening at first but soon realized Betsy was having another baby. She said. "Mr. Click, you have twins. This one is a boy." Joseph Levi was stunned and excited all at once. He could hardly believe he had two babies.

Finally, Ruby helped Betsy clean up and put on a new gown. She propped her up in the bed with two big pillows behind her head. After the midwife cleaned Betsy up and made sure she was ok, she took one baby at a time and bathed it in a big tub of warm water. She wrapped her up with a small warm blanket and laid her in the crib Joseph Levi had built. Then she took the other baby away from Joseph Levi and bathed him in the same tub of warm water. Afterwards, she wrapped the baby boy in a warm blanket and looked at Joseph Levi and asked. "Mr. Click, where are we going to lay this baby?"

Joseph Levi decided to empty a drawer from the dresser and put a heavy blanket in it. He then took the baby boy and laid him in the dresser drawer. He looked at the midwife and then at Betsy and said. "Well we weren't exactly thinking we would have two babies. I guess I had better get busy building another crib as soon as I can. I sure wish it would hurry up and get daylight. I can't wait to tell mama and dad. They will be so surprised and excited." He then walked over to the side of the bed and sat down. He took Betsy's hands in his and gave her a kiss on her forehead. He said to her. "Betsy, I am so proud of you. We have a son and a daughter, and they are the most beautiful babies I have ever seen. Thank you for making me a proud father. Now you shut your eyes and go to sleep for a little while. I have a feeling you are going to be a busy little mother come morning."

The babies slept peacefully for almost an hour and then began to get restless and hungry.

Ruby woke Betsy up and told her to prepare to feed the babies. Tired and sleepy, Betsy forced herself to sit up in bed. She handed her one of the babies to nurse. This was the first time she had a chance to really see the babies. She looked down at its little face and said. "What are we going to name you, little one?" Joseph Levi said to her. "What about Jacob Samuel and Emma Louise?"

"Yes, those are strong respectable names for our son and daughter. I love them and so it should be Emma and Jacob; what lovely names.

Chapter Fifty-Six

As soon as daylight broke, Joseph Levi dressed and went out to the barn and hitched old Ralph up to his carriage. He proceeded up the dirt road to the farm. It was almost six am, but he knew his dad would be up getting ready for his day in the shop. As he approached the farmhouse, he saw his dad walking across the yard. He called his dad and said. "Guess what dad?

We have two babies, a boy and a girl. They were born around four am this morning." Levi was so excited and ran over to congratulate Joseph Levi. "Son, I am so delighted for you and I know your mama is going to be overjoyed with the news. Better get in there and tell her."

Joseph Levi climbed out of the carriage and walked up to the back door with Levi. Sara Jane was in the kitchen preparing breakfast for the family. He approached his mama with a big hug and said. "Guess what, mama? Betsy had twins at four o'clock this morning. A boy and a girl." Sara Jane was beside herself and gave him a big hug. "Oh, Joseph Levi, I am so proud and happy for you and Betsy. I must hurry and finish breakfast so I can go see my new grandbabies. I can't wait to tell Betty Anne."

The midwife took the baby from Betsy and placed him inside the drawer. She then picked up the other baby and placed her in Betsy's arms. Betsy nursed her and cuddled her to her chest. Ruby said. "I believe Jake and Emma are satisfied now and should sleep for a while. I hear buggies coming down the road. Looks like you are about to have company." Ruby went down to the kitchen to put the kettle on the stove. She needed a cup of tea and knew Betsy should eat something to keep up her strength. After all, she didn't just have a baby, she had two babies.

She sliced some of Betsy's fresh bread with some butter and placed them on a tray. Then poured them a cup of tea. As she started up the stairs, Joseph Levi, Levi and Sara Jane came in the front door. Sara Jane said hello to Ruby and asked if she could help her take the tray up the stairs for her. "You must be tired after a long night of delivering two babies." As they walked into the bedroom, Betsy was sitting up in bed. Sara Jane and Levi went over to her and gave her a hug. "We are so proud of you Betsy. Ruby has made you a cup of tea and brought you some of your fresh bread. You drink your tea while I look at my new grandbabies."

She looked down into the cradle, Joseph Levi had made, and tears began to swell up in her eyes. "Oh, my goodness, just look at this beautiful child." She walked over to the dresser and looked down at the other baby. "Oh, Levi, look at this baby, he is precious. Joseph Levi, they are the most beautiful babies I have ever seen. We are so proud for you and Betsy, son." The three of them gathered around Betsy as Joseph Levi began to pray. *"Dear Lord, thank you for these two blessings you have bestowed upon Betsy and me. Help us to be good parents to Jacob (Jake) and Emma and may they grow in your love and peace. Amen."*

Levi said to Sara Jane. "Remember the cradle I made for Joseph Levi before he was born? Why don't I retrieve it from the attic and bring it for the baby? Then they will have a crib for both babies."

"That's a wonderful idea Levi." Replied Sara Jane. Joseph Levi thought so too and said he would go back to the farm later and get it. Sara Jane said. "You, Samuel John and now little Jake and Emma will sleep in the cradle Levi made. Mervin is the only one that hasn't slept in that cradle. I am a proud grandmama today; as she started to cry again.

Sara Jane and Levi decided to leave so Betsy and the babies could sleep. She said. "I will come back this evening with dinner."

"Thank you, mama, you are the best. I will ride over later and pick up the cradle for little Jake." Sara Jane and Levi climbed inside their carriage and urged the horse to head down the dirt road. As they approached the farm, Cindy and Daisy ran out the front door to greet them. Cindy cried out to them. "Is everything ok, mama? Did the baby arrive alright?" Sara Jane put her arms around Cindy and Daisy and told them about Jake and Emma.

The two girls were excited and started talking as fast as they could. "I will let Samuel, Jacob and Samuel John know about the babies. I think Jacob is going to be very proud to know little Jake is named after him."

"And Samuel John too, don't forget." Replied Sara Jane. Levi drove the carriage to the barn and unhitched the horse. He couldn't wait to tell everyone about the babies. "Well boys we have two new grandbabies now. Betsy had twins, this morning. A boy and a girl."

"The boys all laughed and patted each other on the back. Samuel John said. "Oh, my goodness, dad, that must have been something. I bet Joseph Levi is excited."

"We all are son."

Levi decided he would let Joseph Levi tell them what he named the babies. He thought it would be better coming from him. Sara Jane cooked two chicken casseroles for dinner. She would bake one for her family's dinner and one for Betsy and Joseph Levi.

Recipe for Chicken Casserole

Boil a cup of white rice
Boil a large chicken breast
Sautee' onions, green peppers in butter
Combine cream of chicken soup with onions peppers, salt and pepper and 1 cup
  of sour cream
Cut chicken into small pieces and combine with mixture. Pour rice into mixture
Add a cup of cheddar cheese. In a separate bowl, crumble Ritz crackers with
  melted butter and add more cheddar cheese. (can use breadcrumbs to
  substitute crackers)
Combine all the mixture together, and sprinkle the cracker crumbs over the top
  of the casserole
Bake in oven for 45 minutes on 350 degrees

Chapter Fifty-Seven

The following day, Sara Jane couldn't wait to call Betty Anne and tell her about the twins. As soon as she finished with breakfast, she ran down the road to the outdoor phone booth.

Betty Anne was resting in her favorite chair reading a book when the phone rang. When she picked up the phone, it was Sara Jane. "Betty Anne, you are not going to believe this, but Betsy and Joseph Levi had twins yesterday morning. A boy and a girl. I am so excited and couldn't wait to tell you."

"Oh, my goodness, Sara Jane, that is wonderful news. I have got to get Barbara to bring me out there to see them. What did they name the babies?"

"Joseph Levi named the boy Jacob Samuel after his brothers and of course calls him Jake. Our baby girl is Emma Louise. It's a good strong Amish name. Jake and Emma are the most beautiful babies in the whole community and of course, Mervin is too."

Betty Anne couldn't wait to call Barbara and tell her about the twins. She said. "Barbara, you are not going to believe this, but Joseph Levi and Betsy had twin babies. Jake and Emma, aren't those just the cutest names ever! I want to wait at least a week before going out to see them. I'm sure Betsy needs to get adjusted to her new life now. One baby is hard enough to take care of, but two must be really tiring. Would you mind driving me out to the farm next week?"

Barbara was excited about the twins and said she would love to go out to the farm and see them. "Just let me know when you want to go Betty Anne." The following week, Barbara came over to see Betty Anne. She asked her if she would like to go shopping for the twins. "I need to get the twins a gift before we ride out to see them. Would you like to go shopping today, Betty Anne?"

"Yes, I need to get them a gift too." So, the two women drove into Ruby Hope and had a fun day shopping for the babies.

Betty Anne couldn't walk a lot before giving out of breath, so they decided to stop at a local café and have lunch. While they were eating a sandwich and chips and enjoying a hot cup of latte', the mayor of Ruby Hope Valley walked into the café. He recognized Barbara and Betty Anne sitting in the corner of the sandwich shop. He walked over to them and began a conversation. Mr. Watkins said. "Hi ladies, how are you doing today?"

"Hello Mr. Mayor, we are just fine. Would you like to join us for lunch?"

"As a matter of fact, I would."

The Mayor asked Betty Anne how she was doing since she had retired from the orphanage?"

"I really do miss it, but I knew it was time for me to hand the responsibilities over to my best friend Barbara. She has been doing a wonderful job for those children."

"Yes, she has. Mrs. White over there, says the children miss you and want you to come back."

"No, I can't do that, my health has gone downhill and the doctors say I need to rest as much as I can now.

You know, Mr. Mayor, there comes a time in everyone's life when they must give up things. They may not want to, but life has a way of catching up to you and you don't have a choice."

"Yes, of course you are right. I understand and respect you for it." Betty Anne thought to herself, "He has a smile that is so genuine and lights up his face." The Mayor told Betty Anne and Barbara he had an appointment and must be leaving.

"Betty Anne, it has been an honor to see you today. Both you women are remarkable ladies and I hope to see you again soon. Y'all take care." As he walked out of the Café, he turned and waved to them. Barbara said to Betty Anne. "Well that was a surprise and what a nice man he was."

"Yes, he was." The women finished their lunch and decided it was time to head home.

Barbara could tell her friend was tired and needed to rest. She helped Betty Anne into the house and said if she needed her, to please call her.

As Betty Anne dosed off, she thought to herself, "What a nice day it has been. And to see Mr. Watkins, the Mayor of Ruby Hope made it an even better day." *As she slept, she began to dream about Danny. She saw him running up a steep hill with a striped kite in his hand. She was running behind him laughing. He had on shorts and a blue polo shirt. He was barefoot and having such a good time that day. As the kite got higher and higher, he became more excited and started yelling for his mother to come and see. She was running toward him when she suddenly woke up. It had been such an emotional dream that she woke up crying uncontrollable. She missed her son so much she decided to get up and call Sadie. She needed to hear her daughter's voice on the phone. She felt a sadness sweep over her like the world was spinning or seemed to slow down.*

Chapter Fifty-Eight

Barbara decided she would go to the Mayor's office and talk to him about Betty Anne. It had been a couple of weeks since she saw him at the Café; and she figured this was a good time to try and catch him in his office. Mayor Watkins asked Barbara to have a seat. They spoke of all the good works Betty Anne had done for the town and the Amish Community over the past twenty years. "Mr. Watkins, I have been wanting to speak with you about having a town celebration for Betty Anne. She has done so much for this town and the children's orphanage. I think the people of Ruby Hope would want to show their love and appreciation for this woman."

The Mayor sat back in his big overstuffed leather chair and rubbed his hand across his face. "You know Barbara, I have been thinking this very same thing. I just wasn't sure how to go about setting it in motion. Do you have any ideas?" Barbara spoke up and said. "Yes, I do and all I need is your permission to proceed."

"Oh, there is no doubt in my mind this woman is worthy of our gratitude. You just let me know what you need from me; and go ahead and get things rolling. I would like to do this before the cold weather approaches."

Barbara was so grateful to the Mayor and thanked him for his time. She said. "I will be in touch with you soon; and let you know how things are progressing."

"Barbara, have you thought of a date for this event?"

"Well I need to speak with the store managers first and I will get back to you as soon as I can on the celebration date." The Mayor got up from his chair to shake her hand. "You are a wonderful friend to Miss Betty Anne, and I hope everything goes just as you plan."

Barbara left the Mayor's office with a sense of pride and excitement. She knew it was going to be a lot of work bringing the town together for Betty Anne, but she was determined to do it. She decided she would call Sadie and let her know what she had planned. She thought she could assist her in the planning. Maybe she would have some ideas she hasn't thought about.

The following day, Barbara went next door to check on Betty Anne. She wanted to make sure, she was ok. She had also been having a lot of dreams about Danny and seemed upset. As she knocked on Betty Anne's front door, she noticed the door was unlocked and half open. She pushed the door open and called out to her. Betty Anne was asleep on her bed. Barbara woke her up and asked if she was ok. She seemed to be in daze as she sat up in bed. "Yes, I'm ok, is something wrong Barbara?" "I found the front door unlocked and open."

"Oh, my goodness, I must have been tired last night. I guess I forgot to lock the door."

Barbara was very concerned about Betty Anne and offered to take her to the doctor. "No, I'm fine, just a little forgetful. I won't let that happen again. You go ahead and do whatever you have to do today, Barbara, I will be ok."

"Please give me a call if you need me. I will come back later this afternoon to check on you." As she left Betty Anne, she decided she would call Sadie and tell her what was going on. She started thinking out loud, "She needs to come to Ruby Hope and visit her mother, and I need her to help me plan the celebration, too."

That evening Barbara decided to call Sadie. "Hi Sadie, this is Barbara. How are you and Emily Grace doing?"

"We are just fine Barbara. Is anything wrong?" Well, your mother has been having a lot of dreams about Danny lately. She also seems to be very forgetful. She left her front door unlocked and standing open last night. I am really worried about her."

"I am so glad you called me Barbara. I have been worried about her too and have decided to come to Ruby Hope for a visit. Maybe I can convince her to go to the doctor. She may be going into depression again."

"I think that is a good idea, Sadie. She needs you. I also wanted to talk to you about something else. I have spoken with the town Mayor about having a big celebration to honor Betty Anne for all her good work through the years. Especially the years she has spent finding homes for all the orphan children." Sadie was delighted to hear this. "What a wonderful idea Barbara. I would love to help you with the plans."

The following week Sadie reserved two seats on a flight to Pennsylvania. Sadie wanted to surprise her mother. She knew if she told her they were coming; she would clean and cook. She didn't want her getting exhausted. When they finally arrived at Betty Anne's home, Sadie and Emily Grace tapped on her front door. When she opened the door and saw them, she was too excited to speak. Tears started to run down her face as she hugged them both at the same time.

When she was finally able to speak she asked Sadie, "Why didn't you tell me you were coming?"

"We wanted to surprise you, mother."

They had a delightful dinner that evening. After Emily Grace decided to go to bed, Sadie and Betty Anne sat up for hours talking. "Sadie, I have been having dreams about Danny a lot lately. In fact, almost every night for the past week. I wake up crying and don't have the ability to go back to sleep. Sometimes I sleep too much." Sadie noticed the dark circles under her mothers' eyes. It broke her heart to see her this way. Betty Anne continued to say; I have even been forgetful about some things."

"Mother, I am so sorry to hear this. Barbara told me about the front door. You know you need to be more careful about things like that.

I would like for you to go see the doctor while I am here. Maybe he can give you something to help you sleep better."

"Alright, Sadie, I will call in the morning and make an appointment." The doctor gave Betty Anne a prescription to help her sleep. "I think she is experiencing depression, but I believe she will pull out of this after she has had time to rest at night without the dreams. Sometimes people have a relapse of depression after months or even years when they lose a loved one. The memories tend to flood their minds and it's hard to function under such circumstances. They even become a little forgetful at times.

"She is going to be ok; she just needs a little time to adjust to her new lifestyle. She is officially retired from any volunteering or work outside the home. She's not used to staying at home. She has always been an active lady and involved in so many things. Just give her time to heal."

Chapter Fifty-Nine

Sadie and Emily Grace stayed in Ruby Hope for two weeks. Sadie wanted to make sure her mother was going to be ok before she left to go back to New York. While she was in town, she decided to get together with Barbara and start the plans for the town celebration. While they were having breakfast one morning, Sadie said. "Emily Grace is going to stay with you today while I go into town. I have some business to take care of while I am here. Maybe you two could work in your beautiful garden, mother?"

"Yes, of course, it would be nice to have Emily Grace help me."

"I would love to help you grandmama."

Sadie and Barbara drove into Ruby Hope. They each took a place of business and spoke with the managers. Everyone in town was receptive to the idea of a celebration to honor Betty Anne. Many of the people of Ruby Hope had adopted or were fostering the children from the home. They all knew of her tireless work she did at the foster home. Sadie and Barbara decided on a date for everyone to start decorating the town. There would be a big banner made furnished by the town Mayor, Mr. Watkins. The banner would read:

"Celebrating Betty Anne Miller's lifetime of Accomplishments and Loyalty to the Children of Ruby Hope Valley."

Sadie was so proud of her mother. When she saw the banner, she began to cry. Barbara hugged Sadie and said, "Your mother is a wonderful person with the biggest heart I have ever seen. She is so worthy of this celebration. I mean to have this day of honor the most fantastic day this town has ever seen before."

"Thank you, Barbara, I will help you as much as I can and if you need any money, please let me know. I am willing to do anything I can for my dear mother."

Barbara and Sadie paid a visit to the Mayor's office the next day. The three of them decided on a date for the celebration. "What did you ladies think of the banner I had made?"

"It is wonderful Mr. Mayor, thank you for your support of my mother."

"At my last board meeting, I told everyone I wanted this celebration to be the biggest we have ever had before. I also want to invite the Amish community too. Miss Betty Anne has been such a good friend to them and loves them like family, it would be a shame for them not to be invited." Both women agreed with the Mayor and told him they would work hard to make that day a day no one would forget.

Barbara, Sadie and Mayor Watkins settled on August 21st. It was already the middle of July. The women only had four weeks to get the town ready. Sadie said she was going out to the farm to pay Sara Jane and Levi a visit. "I want to tell them all about the celebration for mother and hope they will encourage the Amish community to attend."

"That's a great idea, in the meantime, I am going to the local high school and talk to the band teacher. I want the band to play while marching down the middle of Ruby Hope Valley."

Sara Jane was delighted to see Sadie and wondered where Betty Anne was. She explained about the celebration they were having in town for her. "That is a wonderful idea, Sadie. I know we will be there, and I am sure Joseph Levi and Betsy will come and bring the twins. Jacob will surely be there too."

"Sara Jane, do you think Jacob and Joseph Levi would be willing to say a few words about Betty Anne?"

"Well, I'm not sure Sadie, but I will ask them and see."

I'm going to give you my mobile number and if they will, can you call me and let me know? We don't have a lot of time left. I'm going to have to go back to New York at some point, but I will be back for the celebration." "Of course, Sadie, I understand. I know you have a job in the city. Even us Amish people know how important that is to you city folks."

"Well, I won't have one for long if I don't get back to it."

Sadie felt good about her mother's Amish family now. She thought to herself, "I just hope the boys will be willing to say a few words on mother's behalf. It would mean so much to her." In the meantime, Barbara had visited all the storekeepers and arranged their part in the celebration. Everyone in the town of Ruby Hope would help with the decorations and the parade.

She felt good about everything now and knew her friend Betty Anne was worthy of such a celebration. She had done so much good for this town and the orphan children.

I wonder if I could get in touch with some of the older children. I could see if they would be willing to speak at the forum on her behalf. I think I will go over to the orphanage and speak with Becky White, the Administrator." Becky was busy at her desk as usual when Barbara tapped on the door. "Come in Barbara, how are you?"

"Hi Becky, just wanted to let you know about the town celebration we are going to have for Betty Anne.

It's scheduled for August 21st. I was wondering if you could speak at the forum for her.

The town really wants to honor her for all her years of service helping the children at the orphanage. And other works she has done over the past twenty years." "Well, of course I will, I would be honored to speak on Betty Anne's behalf. She has been an inspiration to all these kids through the years. And we shouldn't forget about the adoption of Jacob, Cindy and Daisy to the Amish family. You can count on me Barbara."

"Becky, do you think any of the other older children that she found homes for would be willing to speak on her behalf, also?"

"I am sure I can round up a few of the kids. Don't worry Barbara, the children will be there."

"Thank you Becky for supporting our cause for Betty Anne.

I will be in touch with you closer to the date. Thanks again, I guess I had better be going now. I know how busy you are."

Chapter Sixty

It was finally time for Sadie and Emily Grace to leave Ruby Hope Valley and return to New York. Sadie needed to speak with her supervisor and husband about returning to Ruby Hope on August 21st for the celebration. Betty Anne was sad to see them leave but was grateful for the time she had with them. They had spent almost three weeks with her, and she loved every minute of it. She was feeling much better now, and the dreams had ceased.

As they hugged and said their goodbye's, Sadie said. "Mother, I will be back soon. So, I want you to stay busy with your garden and get plenty of rest. No more bad dreams. If you feel sad, call us and we will talk about it. I love you mother and will see you again soon." Emily Grace hugged her grandmama and said she loved her too. Betty Anne began to tear up as they got into the taxi to go to the airport. As she turned to walk back into the house, she felt sadness flow over her. She had a distant empty stare. Suddenly Barbara called her name as she snapped out of the gloomy feeling she was experiencing.

"Hi Barbara, Sadie and Emily Grace just left for the airport. Sadie had to get back to her job."

"I know, but she will return soon. In the meantime, you have me. Why don't we drive out to see Sara Jane and the babies? We haven't been out to the Amish community in several weeks now."

"Oh, Barbara, I would love to go see all of them." Barbara and Sadie had all the details of the festivities taken care of. Now she could relax a little. She didn't want Betty Anne depressed again, so she decided she would keep her as busy as she could.

Betty Anne was so grateful to Barbara for taking her to the farm to see her Amish family.

They had a delightful drive in the country. The Amish men and sons were working in the fields and waved to them as they passed by.

Barbara had cautioned Sara Jane not to mention the celebration day. Even if Betty Anne knew about it, she had not said a word and Barbara didn't want to tell her about it just yet.

Sara Jane was in the kitchen baking as usual when they drove up into the yard. She ran to the door with a big smile on her face. She held the screen door open and asked them to come in.

They sat down in the sitting room while she put a kettle of water on the stove. She offered them a cup of tea while they sat and talked. Sara Jane spoke about the three grandchildren. "Betty Anne, I wish you could see Mervin. Can you believe he is trying to walk. And the twins are the cutest little things you have ever seen. They are all doing so well."

"I can't wait to see them, Sara Jane.

I bet they are growing like a weed." Sara Jane wasn't sure what that meant but smiled anyway."

Suddenly, the tea kettle made a loud whistle sound. Sara Jane got up to go pour the tea.

As they drank the tea, they continued to talk about the kids. "I want to hear all about the children.

How is Samuel John doing these days? Is he still helping Levi in the shop? When does Daisy get home from school?"

"Cindy has gone to walk Daisy home from school. They should be home in a few minutes. You will get to see them soon." It wasn't long before the two girls came in the front door.

Betty Anne was amazed at how pretty and grown up they looked. They saw Betty Anne and Barbara and ran over to them and gave them a hug. "It has been so wonderful seeing the girls. They are so pretty and polite."

"Yes, they have been such a comfort to me and Levi. They were so helpful when Samuel John got sick. Both girls would come home from school and play games with him and roll him around in his wheelchair. Cindy would always read a story to him at night before bed. He really enjoyed the reading. Oh, I have some wonderful news about Samuel John I want to share. Doctor Huddleston gave us some news about him the other day."

Betty Anne could hardly wait to hear what she had to say. "What was it Sara Jane?"

"He said Samuel John's blood work was perfect and he should be able to walk without his cane one day soon." Betty Anne was so happy for the family and reached over and gave Sara Jane a hug.

She said. "That just goes to show you prayer does work, and God is always listening. You know, Sara Jane, I have worried myself sick over that boy. I have prayed for him to be able to ride Abby again one day. And now I know he will."

Sara Jane replied, "I just know he will ride the horse again. Sometimes I find him walking around the house without his cane. I think he forgets about it. I'm still so grateful to you for bringing Jacob, Cindy and Daisy into our lives. Even after all these years. I love them as if I had given birth to them."

"I knew these kids would bring sunshine into your lives. I made a good decision the day I took you to the orphanage to meet them. I just knew in my heart they would be coming home with you. You know it's good to remember the good times in life."

"Yes, it is. The years sure have gone by fast, and I can hardly believe how they have grown."

"I want to stop by the shop, Barbara. I would like to see Levi and the rest of the boys."

Sara Jane said she would walk them down to the shop. As they walked into the shop, Jacob and Samuel John saw Betty Anne and went over and gave her a hug. "It is so good to see y'all. Samuel John do you still have that compass I gave you?"

"Yes mam. I carry it everywhere I go."

I just heard the wonderful news about you, Samuel John. I hope to see you riding Abby again one day soon." Samuel John said. "Maybe I will surprise you and the family one of these days."

"I sure hope so, son. I worry about you all the time."

Betty Anne turned to Jacob and asked him how his baby boy was doing? Sara Jane said he was trying to walk already."

"Yes, mam, he is. He is growing so fast."

"We need to go, but I would love to see all the babies soon."

"Levi spoke up and said. "We have missed seeing you, Betty Anne. How have you been?"

"I'm doing ok. I just had a visit from Sadie and Emily Grace.

I am so happy I got to see all of you. I will come back soon." She hugged everyone goodbye as Barbara cranked the car.

Barbara was relieved that no one said a word about the celebration coming up. The two women had a pleasant drive home that afternoon. Betty Anne said. "Thank you for taking me out to see the family, Barbara. I really enjoyed seeing all of them. The girls have grown so much since I last saw them. And Jacob and Samuel John have grown into fine looking young men. I am so proud of all of them."

"I can tell how much they love you and respect you. You have truly been a good friend to all of them." Betty Anne had a radiant glow as she smiled with adoration and pride.

Early one fall morning in August, Sara Jane had gone outside to sweep off the front porch. It was Saturday and everyone else was asleep. She often got up early and did chores around the house before the family got up. This morning was an exception. She glanced over at the barn and noticed someone saddling a horse. She realized it was Samuel John and wondered what he was doing. As she stood there with the broom in her hand, she noticed Samuel John pulled himself up onto the horse. She was horrified at first but soon was relieved. She knew her youngest son was well at last. Off he rode into the fields without a care in the world.

Chapter Sixty-One

It was August eighteenth and the town of Ruby Hope Valley was all abuzz with excitement about the celebration for Betty Anne. Several of the men brought their ladders and hung the banner up right in the center of town. The stores in town were all decorated inside and out for the festivities. Barbara called Sadie and told her things were coming together at last. She asked Sadie when she would be arriving back in town. Sadie said. "Emily Grace and I should be there on the twentieth. I wish I could get there sooner Barbara, but I just can't get off work."

"I understand, Sadie. I look forward to seeing you on the twentieth. Your mother is really going to be surprised. I have tried my best to keep her from going into town. Thankfully she hasn't said anything about going shopping."

"Oh, that's a good thing.

We want her to be surprised if possible." Betty Anne had no idea what was going on. She didn't know Sadie and Emily Grace were coming back to see her so soon, either. So, when they arrived on the twentieth, she couldn't believe it. "I am so happy to see you again so soon. Did you get more vacation time off, Sadie?"

"I did mother and I wanted to spend it with you."

That evening, Betty Anne and Sadie cooked a delicious dinner of roast chicken, boiled potatoes and string beans. After dinner, they sat and talked of old times. Emily Grace was tired after the trip and decided to go to bed. Sadie said. "Don't forget tomorrow is a big day Emily Grace. So, get plenty of rest tonight."

The following day, Sadie got up early and got dressed. After breakfast, she asked her mother if she would like to go into town and have lunch at one of those nice café's?" Betty Anne said. "That sounds like a wonderful idea. Maybe we could ask Barbara to join us. I'll give her a call and ask her?" Sadie began thinking to herself, "Mrs. White and the children from the orphanage were all coming today. Jacob has decided to speak on behalf of mother. Two or three of the adopted children said they would speak at the celebration also." The pride Sadie felt with a gleam in her eyes followed by a satisfied smile was apparent.

Betty Anne gave Barbara a call after breakfast. She told her Sadie and Emily Grace were there and planned to take her to lunch. "We were wondering if you would like to join us?"

"I would love to Betty Anne, but I have an appointment in town today and I must be on my way.

Thank you for asking me, maybe another time." Barbara was leaving to go to town as soon as she hung up the phone with Betty Anne.

After Barbara arrived in town she began gathering everyone together. She thought to herself, "There would be the Mayor of Ruby Hope, two of the adopted children would speak along with Jacob and Joseph Levi. Betty Anne will be so proud and excited to see everyone here to celebrate her achievements and successes. Even though she would want to turn the attention away from herself."

As Sadie, Emily Grace and Betty Anne drove into town, they could see the crowd of people gathered there. "What do you think is going on in town Sadie?" How are we going to get through this crowd of people?" Sadie didn't respond to her and parked the car. When they opened the door, Barbara and a crowd of people surrounded Betty Anne. Everyone was hugging her and saying how grateful they were to her. She had a look of surprise on her face and stuttered when she spoke. Barbara and the Mayor came over and took her by her arm and lead her to the podium. They sat her down and told her this day was for her. She was in shock and couldn't speak.

Mayor Watkins walked up to the podium and asked for everyone's attention. He continued to say to the crowd:

"Good day everyone. I am so happy to see so many people here today to honor this wonderful woman, Betty Anne Miller. For the past twenty years, this lady has been an inspiration to all that live in Ruby Hope Valley. She has worked tirelessly over the years to help and support the local orphanage here in our state of Pennsylvania. She has found many homes for our lost children. I see many of them here today to pay their respects to this lovely lady. She has nursed many of the sick for our local Amish Community as well as people from

our town of Ruby Hope. Betty Anne Miller has never met a stranger that she didn't become a friend of. This day is to Celebrate her."

The Mayor handed Betty Anne a beautiful plaque with an engraved message on it that read:

To Betty Anne Miller

A Remarkable Woman with a big Heart

Whose selfless works have touched everyone she meets. She will always be remembered as an advocate for our Children and a friend of The Amish Community

Betty Anne rose from her seat and stood in front of the podium as the Mayor handed her this beautiful plaque. She had tears rolling down her face as she received the gift. She could barely speak as she said to the crowd:

Thank you everyone for this wonderful gift of love. I am not worthy of all this attention today. I only did what I did for these children because I loved them all and wanted them to have a good home. Whatever I did was from my heart and soul and never from any selfish acts. I pray that all lost children will find a loving home and never be abused again. Thank you again everyone for all the support you have given our Foster Care System and the local orphanage.

Ruby Hope Valley will always be remembered as the little town with a big heart.

The crowd started clapping and yelling how much they loved her. She sat down as Jacob came up to the podium to speak. He spoke into the microphone, "I was one of those abused children. I would not be here today if it wasn't for this wonderful, sweet lady. She gave my two sisters and myself our lives back to us. She found us a loving home with loving parents. I 'm Amish and love the life I have made with this Amish family. I wouldn't have it any other way."

He turned to Betty Anne and said, "I love you with all my heart and will never forget you for all you have done for us. Thank you, Miss Betty Anne." Jacob went over and gave her a hug before he left the podium.

Betty Anne was so moved by Jacobs speech she couldn't stop the tears. She reached into her purse and got a handkerchief out to wipe the tears away. Then she saw Joseph Levi come up to the podium. He walked over to her and hugged her and said to her, "I love you, Miss Betty Anne." Then he spoke into the microphone.

"I am here today because of Betty Anne Miller. When I was just four years old, I was very sick. This lady had become good friends with my mother Sara Jane Click. She noticed how sick I was and advised my mother and father to take me to a doctor she knew. My father was reluctant at first but soon agreed because it wasn't the Amish way. Betty Anne took the time to take me and my mother to a real doctor and found out that I had kidney failure. My father, Levi Click, gave me one of his kidney's.

If it had not been for Betty Anne Miller, I could have died. She has been a big influence in my life. She has helped me to develop my character and encouraged me to go after my dream of being a veterinarian. I love her and thank her for giving me my life back."

He walked over and gave her another hug. She was so emotional over Joseph Levi and Jacobs speeches, that she couldn't speak. She felt like her body had left her and was floating around somewhere else. She was embarrassed for being the center of attention and couldn't believe all of this was happening to her. She thought to herself... "I don't deserve all of this attention. I did what I did because my heart told me to." Sadie spoke to her and brought her out of her thoughts. "Mother, you have had an exciting day. Why don't we go enjoy all the activities that are going on. I think there are a few more people that would like to speak to you."

Chapter Sixty-Two

Sadie took her mother's arm and helped her down the steps of the podium. She stopped to thank Mayor Watkins for this day. She said. "Mayor Watkins I just want to thank you for this wonderful day. It has been an emotional day for me, but I have enjoyed every minute of it. I don't feel that I am deserving of all of this."

"You are so welcome Miss Betty Anne. I don't know of any other person that is more deserving than you are. You are a public tribute to our little town with a big heart."

There were all kinds of activities going on in town that day. Many of the adopted and fostered children were there to show their appreciation for her. Standing off to the side of the crowd, there were several children whom she had found loving homes for. She walked over to them as they all surrounded her and began to hug her. She was so happy to see them as the tears started again. "Y'all will have to forgive me for being so emotional but just seeing all these happy children makes my heart sing."

Each one of them looked healthy and happy. She felt at that moment she had done something good in her life that made a difference. Sara Jane and Levi were there waiting to speak to her. Joseph Levi had brought Betsy and the twins, Emma and Jake. She also saw many of the Amish ladies she had gotten to know at the quilting group. She was happy to see everyone and walked over to speak to them. Sara Jane gave her a big hug and said how proud she was of her. "I am so happy to see all of you here today. This would not have meant very much to me without all of you."

"We would not have missed this for the world, replied Sara Jane."

Levi and Sara Jane said their goodbye's and left to go home. They didn't participate in any activities; as was their way. Betty Anne knew in her heart that she had the best of two worlds. She had a wonderful daughter and granddaughter. Her friend and neighbor, Barbara was the best friend anyone could ever have. But most of all, she had her Amish family. They were the most loving, thoughtful and caring people she had ever known. They excepted her with open hearts. They trusted her and believed in her and were always there for her. She knew she couldn't ask God for anything more.

After arriving home, she was drained of her mental resources. Sadie encouraged her to lie down and rest for a while. Sadie said. "I will cook dinner while you rest, and I will wake you up when it's ready." Betty Anne didn't give Sadie any argument about lying down. Before she dozed off to sleep, she said a silent prayer.

"Dear kind heavenly father, I want to thank you for today. I want to thank you for giving me a lifetime of good friends and family. Without them I would have been lost forever. You gave me my daughter back and the strength to carry on. It was difficult at times Lord, but you gave me a reason to live and help others. I hope I am deserving of all the children I tried to help through the years. I know they are better off now with families instead of having to live their lives without someone to love them. You also gave me a second family whom I love dearly. My Amish family has helped me through the years to become a better person and know that I was loved when I thought I had lost my daughter and son. They invited me into their homes and loved me unconditionally. Thank you for a road well-traveled. I know I could not have traveled that road without you beside me. Thank you for loving me. Amen."

The following day, Sadie and Emily Grace left Ruby Hope Valley to return to their home in New York. Betty Anne was sad to see them go but knew in her heart she would see them again soon. They said their goodbye's as the taxi arrived to take them the airport in Lancaster. '

She was so relieved when they arrived home without any incident's on the plane. She sat down in her favorite recliner and thought about the celebration and her life as she dozed off to sleep.

Betty Anne would go on living her life as the good lord wanted her too. She was a good friend to everyone she met. She was visited by her neighbors and her Amish family often. Joseph Levi and Betsy would come to see her often and bring the twins. Jacob and Grace would bring Mervin by to see her each time they were in town. Sara Jane and Barbara continued to visit and help her with her chores and garden. She was happy to see them each time they stopped by.

One afternoon, she wasn't feeling well, so she decided to lay down for a short nap. She was thinking about all the good times she had in her life. She thought of Sadie and Emily Grace and wondered what they were doing. She wished they would come to visit her soon. She wondered if Sara Jane and Barbara were coming today. She suddenly falls asleep. She dreamed of all her friends and Amish family. She slept almost three hours because she was so tired.

She decided she would get up and go outside to work in her garden. She started thinking about her life as she pulled weeds from the ground. She thought she had lost her children forever, but God gave her a second chance. She lost her son Danny and that was something she could never get over. She missed him so much. But God gave her back her daughter, Sadie. Since Sadie was back in her life; she had been the most loving daughter anyone could ever ask for. He also gave her Sara Jane, who has always been like a daughter to her. They had a bond of friendship that has lasted for twenty years. They have gone through many ups and downs in their lives: but always together.

She stood up and complained about her back hurting and then thought, "Well I am eighty years old now, no wonder my back aches. But that's ok, the good lord has given me wonderful people to help me along my path; and whatever happens from here on out, I will always be grateful for the time I have left; with no regrets. I am at peace with the world and if I should not wake up tomorrow I know I have left my mark on someone's heart."

She says a silent prayer, "*Thank you Lord for all of your blessings and the wonderful people in my life. Looking back on my life, dear Lord, you gave me the opportunity to help abused children and become best friends with an Amish family, whom I love dearly. Watch over all those kids I helped along the way and give them hope for a bright future. I pray I can continue to encourage and inspire all those I met on my journey. And Lord, thank you for giving me the strength to still work in my garden, Amen.*"

The Amish Way of Life - Written by Marilyn Lot

It's a different kind of life
The way the Amish live giving up so many things
Perhaps they want to give to God and follow His path
Appreciate what's at hand
They cherish what He offers
They plow their fields each year
With a horse-drawn plow
They raise pigs and chickens
We think we don't know how
But we could, don't you think?
Leave out our modern ways
Reap what God has given us
Go back to the olden days
Yes, the Amish way of Life
Is truly exciting to me
A Wonderful way to serve God
For He gives so generously?

Credits

Amish Boy – Ethan T Moss

Amish Boy – Joshua E. Anderson

Amish Girl – Jo Marie Sims

Photography by – Ronda L Moss Photography and Diane W Gordon

Edited by – Randy D Moss/Jerry W Gordon/Diane Williams Gordon

The Best of Amish Cooking Book – Written by Phyllis Good

Recipe: Vegetable Beef Soup

The Best of Amish Cooking Book – Written by Phyllis Good

Recipe: Amish Apple Pie

Amish America Newsletter – On Amish Education

Amish America Newsletter – The Amish Approach to Electricity

Amish America Magazine – Basic Similarities between Amish and
Mennonites

A Poem – The Amish Way of Life – Written by Marilyn Lot

A Poem – The Love of God – Written by Orva Hochstetler – May 1, 2017

Know our Back. Org./Spinal Infections/Patient Education Committee

Prayer for Family Protection – (A Family From www.lords prayer
words.com)

Acknowledgement and Dedication – Written by Diane Williams
Gordon

INDEX

About the Author

Diane Williams Gordon is the author of *Ruby Hope Valley*. She is a native of Atlanta, Georgia where she lives with her husband, Jerry and her dog, Murphy. She loves spending time with family and reading Amish novels. Diane has always been intrigued by the Amish culture and their plain and simple ways of life. She is retired from one of the many Professional Golfers Association of America's club facilities.

Note from the Author

Word-of-mouth is crucial for any author to succeed. If you enjoyed *Return to Ruby Hope Valley* please leave a review online—anywhere you are able. Even if it's just a sentence or two. It would make all the difference and would be very much appreciated.

Thanks!
Diane

Thank you so much for reading
one of Diane Williams Gordon's novels.
If you enjoyed our book, please check out our recommendation
for your next great read!

Ruby Hope Valley by Diane Williams Gordon

Ruby Hope Valley is a delightful and heartwarming book
of love, faith, and friendship.

View other Black Rose Writing titles at
<u>www.blackrosewriting.com/books</u> and use promo code
PRINT to receive a **20% discount** when purchasing.

9 781684 335169